REMAST

REMASTERING is a term usually used in the music and film industries, through which beloved movies and music get cleaned up, streamlined, and enhanced so they can be accessed by a new generation. Similarly, at Remastered Classics, we're excited about bringing the best of classic literature into the hands of modern readers. The classic novels have some of the greatest characters and story lines ever created. Yet, many modern readers struggle with dated vocabulary, long narrative descriptions, and slow build-ups.

Remastered Classics are the classic tales with modern editing techniques applied: the characters and story lines are preserved, outdated vocabulary and concepts are either updated or explained, and lengthy narration and descriptions may be trimmed or turned into live action or dialogue. The Remastered editions are not meant to replace the original stories, but are meant to serve as a bridge, introducing a new generation of readers to the greatness of these works.

We look forward to your getting hooked on Sir Arthur Conan Doyle, Mark Twain, Alexandre Dumas and so many more. Please share with us your reading experience and let us know which classics you would like to see remastered in the near future.

Visit us at *www.ClassicsRemastered.com* and *facebook.com/ClassicsRemastered*.

Copyright © 2012 by Leo Zanav

All rights reserved under International and Pan-American Copyright Conventions. Published in the United States by Classics Remastered, an imprint of Lionstail Press.

Library of congress Cataloging-in-Publication Data

Conan Doyle, Sir Arthur.

A Study in Scarlet

By Sir Arthur Conan Doyle and Leo Zanav

ISBN: 978-1-62393-000-4

LCCN: 2012945030

1. Mystery - Fiction - Sherlock Holmes

SHERLOCK HOLMES REMASTERED

BOOK 1

A STUDY IN SCARLET
A REMASTERED CLASSIC

A NOVEL BY
SIR ARTHUR CONAN DOYLE

REMASTERED BY
LEO ZANAV

CLASSICS REMASTERED
AN IMPRINT OF LIONSTAIL PRESS

CHAPTER I
MR. SHERLOCK HOLMES

"YOU have just returned from Afghanistan, I see."

These were the first words Sherlock Holmes spoke to me, and never in my life did I have a stranger introduction. "How on earth did you know that?" I asked in astonishment.

"It is entirely obvious from looking at you, my good man, that you have just returned to London following an unsuccessful career as an army doctor in Afghanistan."

"Preposterous. No man could tell all that just by looking at me."

"On the contrary, it is quite elementary. The moment I saw you I knew you had come from Afghanistan, because no other explanation could fit. It is clear you are a gentleman of the medical type, but with the air of a military man. Clearly then you must be an army doctor. I know you just came from the tropics because your face is tanned, but your white wrists show that that is not the natural color of your skin. You have undergone hardship and sickness, as your haggard face says clearly. You hold your left arm in a stiff and unnatural manner, showing that you have been injured. I asked myself, where in the tropics could an English doctor have seen hardship and been wounded? Clearly in the recent battles in Afghanistan."

"Quite right. It all seems obvious enough now that you have explained it. But how did you know my career was unsuccessful?"

"From your age, Dr. Watson. You barely look old enough to have completed medical school. I surmised that you must have entered the army directly after receiving your degree and been wounded almost immediately afterwards. I would certainly call such a career unsuccessful."

"Right again," I said, experiencing for the first time the remarkable brains of the most extraordinary man I would ever know.

It was in fact the second time that day that I had discussed my injuries in the army. The first time had occurred only a few hours earlier at a bookstore in the Strand. I had felt a tap on the shoulder and turned to see my old friend Stamford who had started his studies at the University of London Medical School just as I was finishing my own.

"Whatever have you been doing with yourself, Watson?" he asked in undisguised wonder. "You are as thin as a reed and as brown as a nut."

I described to him how I had just barely escaped Afghanistan with my life. I took a bullet in the shoulder which shattered the bone and left me with tremendous blood loss. I only escaped alive thanks to the quick thinking of my assistant, who threw me across the back of a pack horse and rode me safely behind the British lines. My problems were only beginning, however, as my wound got infected and I lay in a military hospital for over month with a high fever.

"And then what happened?" asked Stamford.

"Well, I was too sick for the army, but too healthy for the hospital," I replied. "So they shipped me back here to London to nurse myself back to health."

"Poor Devil! What will you do now? You don't look healthy enough to work."

"On that account the army has been generous. They're giving me a salary of 11 shillings a day for the next year to give me time to recover. It's enough to live on, but not at the hotel I'm currently staying at. So now I'm looking for lodgings, trying to solve the problem of finding comfortable rooms at a reasonable price."

"That's a strange thing," remarked my companion. "You are the second man today that has used that expression to me."

"And who was the first?" I asked.

"A fellow working at the chemical laboratory at the hospital. He was complaining this morning because he could not get someone to split with him in some nice rooms he had found which were too expensive for him alone."

"By Jove!" I cried. "If he really wants someone to share the rooms and the expense, I am the very man for him. I should prefer having a partner to being alone."

Young Stamford looked rather strangely at me. "You don't know Sherlock Holmes yet," he said. "You might not care for him as a constant companion."

"Why? What is there against him?"

"Oh, I didn't say there was anything against him. He is a little queer in his ideas—an enthusiast in some branches of science. However, as far as I know he is a decent fellow."

"A medical student, I suppose?"

"No—I have no idea what he intends to do. I believe he is well up in anatomy, and he is a first class chemist; but, as far as I know, he has never taken any medical classes. His studies are very unusual, but he has built up a tremendous store of out of the way knowledge."

"Did you never ask him what he wanted to do with it?" I asked.

"No; he is not an easy man to get information from, though he can be communicative enough when he feels like it."

"I should like to meet him," I said. "If I am to live with anyone, I should prefer a man who lives quietly. I am not strong enough yet to stand much noise or excitement. I had enough of both in Afghanistan to last me for the remainder of my life. How could I meet this friend of yours?"

"He is sure to be at the chemistry lab," my friend answered. "He either avoids the place for weeks, or else he works there from morning to night. We can take a cab there now if you like."

"Certainly," I answered, and I put out my arm to hail a passing hansom cab. The driver pulled on the reigns, brought the horse to a halt, and we climbed into the carriage.

As we made our way to the lab, Stamford gave me a few more details about Sherlock. "You mustn't blame me if you don't get along with him," he said. "I know nothing more of him than what I've learned from meeting him in the laboratory. This was your idea, so you must not hold me responsible."

"If we don't get along it will be easy to part company," I answered. "It seems to me, Stamford," I added, looking hard at my friend, "that you have some reason for being nervous about this. Does he have an uncontrolled temper or something? Go on, tell me what's bothering you."

"It is not easy to express the inexpressible," he answered with a laugh. "Holmes is a little too scientific for my tastes. I could imagine him giving a friend a little pinch of something he made in the lab just to see how it would effect him. To do him justice, I think that he would take it himself with the same readiness. He seems to have a passion for definite and exact knowledge."

"There's nothing wrong with that."

"True, but he can take it too far. For instance, beating the dead animals in the dissecting room with a stick."

"Beating them with a stick!"

"Yes, to see whether bruises could be made after death. I saw him at it with my own eyes."

"But he is not a medical student?"

"No. I have no idea what he wants to do with his studies. But here we are, and you must form your own impressions about him." As he spoke, we got out of the cab and stepped into the hospital. It was a familiar place to me, and I needed no assistance to find the chemical lab. It was a room with a high roof, filled with countless glass bottles. There was only one student in the room, a young man who was bending over a distant table absorbed in his work. At the sound of our steps he looked around and sprang to his feet with a cry of pleasure. "I've found it! I've found it," he shouted to my friend, running towards us with a test tube in his hand. "I have found a chemical which reacts to blood and nothing else." Had he discovered a gold mine, greater delight could not have shone upon his face.

"Dr. Watson, Mr. Sherlock Holmes," said Stamford, introducing us.

"You have just returned from Afghanistan, I see," he said, beginning the extraordinary discussion that I have already discussed above. However, fascinated as I was by his comments, he was much more eager to return to the subject of his test tubes. "The question now is about hemoglobin. No doubt you see the significance of my discovery?"

"It is interesting, chemically, no doubt," I answered, "but practically—"

"Why, man, it is the most practical medical-legal discovery for years. Don't you see that it gives us a true test for blood stains? Come over here now!" He seized me by the coat sleeve in his eagerness, and drew me over to his table. "Let us have some fresh blood," he said, digging a pin into his finger, and drawing a drop of blood. "Now, I add this small quantity of blood to a liter of water," he demonstrated with a flourish. "You see the mixture still looks like pure water. The blood cannot be more than one part in a million. Yet watch the reaction." As he spoke, he threw in a few white crystals, and then added some drops of a clear fluid. In an instant the water turned a light brown, and what looked like dust fell to the bottom of the glass jar.

"Ha! ha!" he cried, clapping his hands, and looking as delighted as a child with a new toy. "What do you think of that?"

"It seems to be a very delicate test," I remarked.

"Beautiful! beautiful! The old tests were very clumsy and were useless if the blood stains were more than a few hours old. But this test works whether the blood is old or new. Had this test been invented, there are hundreds of men now walking the earth who would long ago have paid the penalty of their crimes."

"Indeed!" I murmured.

"Criminal cases are continually hinging upon that one point. A man is suspected of a crime months perhaps after it has been committed. His clothes are examined, and brownish stains discovered upon them. Are they blood stains, or mud stains, or rust stains, or fruit stains, or what are they? That is a question which has puzzled many an expert, and why? Because there was no reliable test. Now we have the Sherlock Holmes' test, and there will no longer be any difficulty." His eyes fairly glittered as he spoke, and he bowed as if the room were filled with an applauding crowd.

"You are to be congratulated," I remarked, very surprised at his excitement.

"There was the case of Von Bischoff at Frankfort last year. He would certainly have been hanged had this test been in existence. Then there was Mason of Bradford, and the notorious Muller, and Lefevre of Montpellier, and Samson of New Orleans. I could name at least twenty cases in which it would have been decisive."

"You seem to be a walking calendar of crime,"

said Stamford with a laugh. "You might start a paper on those lines. Call it the 'Police News of the Past.'"

"Very interesting reading it might be made, too," remarked Sherlock Holmes, sticking a small bandage over the cut he'd made on his finger. "I have to be careful," he continued, turning to me with a smile, "for I dabble with poisons a good deal." He held out his hand as he spoke, and I noticed that it was covered with many similar injuries.

"We came here on business," said Stamford, sitting down on a high three legged stool, and pushing another one in my direction with his foot. "My friend here wants to take rooms, and as you were complaining that you could get no one to share with you, I thought that I had better bring you together."

Sherlock Holmes seemed delighted at the idea of sharing his rooms with me. "I have my eye on rooms in Baker Street," he said, "which would be perfect for us. I generally have chemicals about, and occasionally do experiments. Would that annoy you?"

"By no means."

"Let me see—what are my other shortcomings? I get in the dumps at times, and don't open my mouth for days on end. Just let me alone, and I'll soon be right. What have you to confess now? It's just as well for two fellows to know the worst of one another before they begin to live together."

I laughed at this cross-examination. "I object to loud noises because my nerves are shaken. I sleep late and am extremely lazy. I have another set of vices when I'm well, but those are the main ones while I'm getting myself back to health."

"Do you include violin playing in your

category of loud noises?" he asked, anxiously.

"It depends on the player," I answered. "A well played violin is a treat—a badly played one—"

"Oh, that's all right," he cried, with a merry laugh. "I think we may consider the thing as settled—that is, if the rooms are agreeable to you."

"When shall we see them?"

"Call for me here at noon tomorrow, and we'll go together and settle everything," he answered.

"All right—noon exactly," said I, shaking his hand.

Stamford and I left him working among his chemicals, and we walked together towards my hotel.

"By the way," I said suddenly, stopping and turning upon Stamford, "that was really something how he knew I had come from Afghanistan!"

"That's just his little peculiarity," he said. "But you got a treat when he explained his reasoning. A good many people would like to know how he finds things out."

"Oh! A mystery is he?" I cried, rubbing my hands. "I am much obliged to you for bringing us together. I look forward to studying his ways."

"You must study him, then," Stamford said, as he bade me good-bye. "You'll find him a knotty problem, though. I'll bet he learns more about you than you about him. Good-bye."

"Good-bye," I answered, and strolled on to my hotel, considerably interested in my new acquaintance.

CHAPTER II
THE SCIENCE OF DEDUCTION

WE met next day as arranged, and inspected the rooms at No. 221B, Baker Street. There were two comfortable bedrooms and a large sitting room, cheerfully furnished, and illuminated by two broad windows. The landlady, Mrs. Hudson, lived below us and included all meals in the price. So desirable in every way were the rooms, and so reasonable was the rent when divided between us, that we took it on the spot. That very evening I moved myself over from the hotel, and on the following morning Sherlock Holmes arrived with several boxes and trunks. For a day or two we were busy unpacking and laying out our things. That done, we gradually began to settle down and accommodate ourselves to our new surroundings.

Holmes was certainly not a difficult man to live with. He was quiet in his ways, and his habits were regular. It was rare for him to be up after ten at night, and he had almost always eaten breakfast and gone out before I rose in the morning. Sometimes he spent his day at the chemical laboratory, sometimes in the dissecting rooms, and occasionally in long walks, which appeared to take him into the lowest portions of the City. Nothing could exceed his energy when the working fit was upon him; but now and again a reaction would seize him. At those times, he would lie upon the sofa in the sitting room, hardly uttering a word or moving a muscle from morning to night.

As the weeks went by, my interest in him and my curiosity as to his aims in life gradually increased. His appearance was striking. He was a bit over six feet tall, but so skinny that he seemed even taller. His eyes were sharp and piercing, except for those brief periods when he lay on the sofa with a dreamy, vacant expression in his eyes. He had a narrow, hawk-like nose that gave his whole expression an air of alertness and decision. His hands were always blotted with ink and stained with chemicals, yet he had an extraordinary delicacy of touch, as I saw whenever he handled his fragile chemistry instruments.

My health was so weak at this time that I rarely went out except when the weather was perfect, and I had few friends in London. Having little else to do, I spent much of my time wondering about Holmes and trying to figure out what his career aspirations were.

He was not studying medicine. He had himself told me so. He was also not working through the coursework of any other degree program. Yet his zeal for certain studies was remarkable, and his knowledge was so extraordinary that his observations astounded me. Surely no man would work so hard unless he had some definite end in view. No man burdens his mind with small matters unless he has some very good reason for doing so.

His ignorance was as remarkable as his knowledge. Of modern literature, philosophy, and politics, he appeared to know next to nothing. Upon my quoting Thomas Carlyle, he asked who he was and what he had done. My surprise reached its peak, however, when I found out that he was ignorant of the makeup of the Solar System. I was shocked that any civilized person in the nineteenth century should not know that the earth travelled around the sun.

"You appear to be astonished," he said, smiling at my expression of surprise. "Now that I do know it I shall do my best to forget it."

"To forget it!"

"You see," he explained, "A man's brain is like an empty attic. You have to put in whatever furniture you choose. A fool takes in everything he comes across, so that there is no room for anything useful to find a place, or else the useful information gets so jumbled up with everything else that he has difficulty laying his hands upon it. Now the skillful workman is very careful as to what he takes into his brain-attic. He will have nothing but the tools which may help him in doing his work, but of these he has a large assortment, and all in the most perfect order. It is a mistake to think that that little room has elastic walls and can grow to any extent. Depend upon it that there comes a time when for every piece of knowledge you add, you forget something that you knew before. It is of the highest importance, therefore, not to have useless facts elbowing out the useful ones."

"But the solar system!" I protested.

"What the deuce is it to me?" he interrupted impatiently; "you say that we go round the sun. If we went round the moon it would not make a penny's worth of difference to me or to my work."

I was on the point of asking him what that work might be, but something in his manner told me that the question would be unwelcome. I thought over our short conversation, however, and tried to draw my deductions from it. He said that he would acquire no knowledge which was not relevant to his objective. Therefore all the knowledge which he possessed must be useful to him. I thought about all the areas in which he was well informed. I even took a pencil and jotted them down. I could not help smiling at the document when I had completed it. It ran in this way—

SHERLOCK HOLMES—his limits.

1. Knowledge of Literature—None
2. Philosophy—None
3. Astronomy—None
4. Politics—Little
5. Botany—Some. Knows about poisons, but nothing of gardening.
6. Geology—Some. Can tell different soils from each other at a glance. After walks has shown me splashes upon his trousers, and told me by their color in what part of London he had received them.
7. Chemistry—Tremendous.
8. Anatomy—Accurate, but unsystematic.
9. Sensational Literature—Immense. He appears to know every detail of every horror done in the century.
10. Plays the violin well.
11. Is an expert boxer and swordsman.
12. Has a good practical knowledge of British law.

When I had got this far in my list I threw it into the fire in despair. "If I can only find what the fellow is driving at by the combination of all these things and discover a job that needs them." I said to myself, "I may as well give up the attempt at once."

During the first week or so we had no visitors, and I had begun to think that my companion was as friendless as I was myself. Before long, however, I found that he had many acquaintances, and from different classes of society. There was one little rat faced, dark eyed fellow who was introduced to me as Mr. Lestrade, and who came three or four times in a single week. One morning a young girl called, fashionably dressed, and stayed for half an hour or more. The same afternoon brought a grey headed visitor, looking like a peddler, who appeared very excited. On another occasion an old white haired gentleman had an interview with my companion; and on another a railway porter in his velveteen uniform. When any of these individuals appeared, Sherlock Holmes would beg me for the use of the sitting room, and I would retire to my bedroom. He always apologized to me for putting me to this inconvenience. "I have to use this room as a place of business," he said, "and these people are my clients." Again I had an opportunity of asking him a point blank question, and again my delicacy prevented me from forcing another man to confide in me. I imagined at the time that he had some strong reason for not telling me what it was, but he soon came around to the subject of his own accord.

It was upon the 4th of March, 1887 as I have good reason to remember, that I arose somewhat earlier than usual, and found that Sherlock Holmes had not yet finished his breakfast. The landlady had become so accustomed to my late habits that my place had not been laid nor my coffee prepared. I rang the bell and let her know that I was ready. Then I picked up a magazine from the table and read it while I waited, as my companion munched silently at his toast. One of the articles had a pencil mark at the heading, and I naturally began to run my eye through it.

Its was titled "The Book of Life," and it attempted to show how much an observant man might learn of all things that came his way. It struck me as being a remarkable mixture of shrewdness and of absurdity. The reasoning was close and intense, but the deductions appeared to me to be far fetched and exaggerated. The writer claimed that by a momentary expression, a twitch of a muscle or a glance of an eye, it is possible to understand a man's innermost thoughts. According to the author, deceit was an impossibility to one trained to observe and analyze; and his conclusions were infallible. Yet, so startling would his results appear to those who didn't know them that they might consider him a magician.

"From a drop of water," said the writer, "a logical man could understand oceans and waterfalls without having ever seen or heard of them. So all life is a great chain, the nature of which is known whenever we are shown a single link of it. Life is not long enough to learn everything about the Science of Deduction and Analysis. One wishing to learn should start simply. When meeting a stranger, he can try to deduce the man's history and profession. By analyzing the man's finger nails, his coat sleeves, his boots, the knees of his pants, the roughness of his hands, his expression—by each of these things a man's trade is plainly revealed."

"What twaddle!" I cried, slapping the magazine down on the table, "I never read such rubbish in my life."

"What is it?" asked Sherlock Holmes.

"Why, this article," I said, pointing at it with my egg spoon as I sat down to my breakfast. "I see that you have read it since you have marked it. I don't deny that it is smartly written. It irritates me though. It is evidently the theory of some arm chair lounger who wrote all these neat little ideas in his own study. It is not practical. I should like to see him in a third class carriage on the Underground, and asked to give the trades of all his fellow travelers. I would lay a thousand to one against him."

"You would lose your money," Sherlock Holmes remarked calmly. "As for the article I wrote it myself."

"You!"

"Yes. I have an eye both for observation and for deduction. The theories which I have expressed there, and which appear to you to be such rubbish are really extremely practical—so practical that I depend upon them for my bread and cheese."

"And how?" I asked involuntarily.

"Well, I have a trade of my own. I suppose I am the only one in the world. I'm a consulting detective, if you can understand what that is. Here in London we have lots of Government detectives and lots of private ones. When these fellows are at fault they come to me, and I manage to put them on the right scent. They lay all the evidence before me, and I am generally able, by the help of my knowledge of the history of crime, to set them straight. There is a strong resemblance about misdeeds, and if you have all the details of a thousand at your fingertips, it is odd if you can't unravel the thousand and first. Mr. Lestrade is a well known detective. He got confused recently over a forgery case, and that was what brought him here."

"And these other people?"

"They are all people who are in trouble about something, and want a little enlightening. I listen to their story, they listen to my comments, and then I pocket my fee."

"But do you mean to say," I said, "that without leaving your room you can unravel some knot which other men can make nothing of, although they have seen every detail for themselves?"

"Quite so. I have a kind of intuition that way. Now and again a case turns up which is a little more complex. Then I have to go and see things with my own eyes. You see, I have a lot of special knowledge which I apply to the problem, and which helps wonderfully. Those rules of deduction laid down in that article you scorned are invaluable to me in practical work. Observation with me is second nature. You appeared to be surprised when I told you, on our first meeting, that you had recently been in Afghanistan."

"It is simple enough as you explained it," I said, smiling. But inside I was thinking that while Sherlock was quite clever, he seemed to have an over-inflated vision of himself.

"There are no crimes and no criminals in these days," he said. "I know well that I have it in me to make my name famous. No man lives or has ever lived who has brought the same amount of study and of natural talent to the detection of crime which I have done. And what is the result? There are no great crimes to detect. At most there's some bungling villainy with a motive so transparent that even the police at Scotland Yard can see through it."

I was growing more annoyed at his style of conversation. I thought it best to change the topic, and got up and walked over to the window. "I wonder what that fellow is looking for?" I asked, pointing to a plainly dressed individual who was walking slowly down the other side of the street, looking anxiously at the numbers. He had a large blue envelope in his hand, and was evidently the bearer of a message.

"You mean the retired sergeant of Marines," said Sherlock Holmes.

"Brag and bounce!" thought I to myself. "He knows that I cannot verify his guess."

The thought had hardly passed through my mind when the man whom we were watching caught sight of the number on our door, and ran rapidly across the road. We heard a loud knock, a deep voice below, and heavy steps ascending the stair.

"For Mr. Sherlock Holmes," he said, stepping into the room and handing my friend the letter.

Here was an opportunity of taking the conceit out of Sherlock. When he made his comment, he little thought I would have a chance to test him. "May I ask, my good man," I said, in the blandest voice, "what your trade may be?"

"Military, sir, retired" he said, gruffly. "My uniform is away for repairs."

"And you were?" I asked, with a slightly nasty glance at my companion.

"A sergeant, sir, Royal Marine Light Infantry, sir. No answer?" He addressed Sherlock, who shook his head. "Right, sir." He clicked his heels together, raised his hand in a salute, and was gone.

CHAPTER III.
THE LAURISTON GARDEN MYSTERY

I confess that I was shaken by this fresh proof of my companion's theories. My respect for his powers of analysis increased wondrously. There still remained some lurking suspicion in my mind, however, that the whole thing was a pre-arranged episode, intended to dazzle me, though what earthly object he could have in doing so I couldn't guess. When I looked at him he had finished reading the note, and his eyes had assumed the vacant, lackluster expression which showed he was thinking hard.

"How in the world did you deduce that?" I asked.

"Deduce what?" said he.

"Why, that he was a retired sergeant of Marines."

"I have no time for trifles," he answered, brusquely; then with a smile, "Excuse my rudeness. You broke the thread of my thoughts; but perhaps it is as well. So you actually were not able to see that that man was a sergeant of Marines?"

"No, indeed."

"It was easier to know it than to explain why I knew it. If you were asked to prove that two and two made four, you might find some difficulty, and yet you are quite sure of the fact. Even across the street I could see a great blue anchor tattooed on the back of the fellow's hand. That smacked of the sea. He had a military walk, however, and a trim beard. Thus he's not an ordinary sailor, but a marine. He was a man with some amount of self-importance and a certain air of command. You must have observed the way in which he held his head and swung his cane. A steady, respectable, middle aged man, too, on the face of him —all facts which led me to believe that he had been a sergeant."

"Wonderful!" I said.

"Commonplace," said Holmes, though I thought from his expression that he was pleased at my evident surprise and admiration. "I said just now that there were no criminals. It appears that I am wrong— look at this!" He threw me the note which the marine had brought.

"Why," I cried, as I cast my eye over it, "this is terrible!"

"It does seem to be a little out of the ordinary," he remarked, calmly. "Would you mind reading it to me aloud? I'd like to get all the details straight in my head."

This is the letter which I read to him:

"MY DEAR MR. SHERLOCK HOLMES,

"There has been a bad business during the night at 3, Lauriston Gardens, off the Brixton Road. A police officer on the beat saw a light there about two in the morning, and as the house was an empty one, suspected that something was amiss. He found the door open, and in the front room, which is bare of furniture, discovered the body of a gentleman, well dressed, and having cards in his pocket bearing the name of 'Enoch J. Drebber, Cleveland, Ohio, U.S.A.' There had been no robbery, nor is there any evidence as to how the man met his death. There are marks of blood in the room, but there is no wound upon his person. We are at a loss as to how he came into the empty house; indeed, the whole affair is a puzzler. If you can come round to the house any time before twelve, you will find me there. I have left everything untouched until I hear from you. If you are unable to come I shall give you fuller details, and would esteem it a great kindness if you would favor me with your opinion. Yours faithfully,

"TOBIAS GREGSON."

"Gregson is the smartest detective in Scotland Yard," my friend remarked. "He and Lestrade are the best of a bad group. They are both quick and energetic, but conventional—shockingly so. They have their knives into one another, too. They are as jealous as a pair of professionals can be. There will be some fun over this case if they are both put upon the scent."

I was amazed at the calm way in which he spoke. "Surely there is not a moment to be lost," I cried. "Shall I go and order you a cab?"

"I'm not sure about whether I will go. I'm in one of my moods, and when like this, I'm the most incurably lazy devils that ever stood in shoe leather."

"Why, it is just such a chance as you have been longing for."

"My dear fellow, what does it matter to me.

Supposing I unravel the whole matter, you may be sure that Gregson, Lestrade, and friends will take all the credit. That comes from being an unofficial detective."

"But he begs you to help him."

"Yes. He knows that I am better than him, and tells me so; but he would cut out his tongue before telling anyone else. However, we may as well go and have a look. I shall work it out on my own. I may have a laugh at them if I have nothing else. Come on!"

He hustled on his overcoat, and moved about in a way that showed that his energy was coming back to him.

"Get your hat," he said.

"You wish me to come?"

"Yes, if you have nothing better to do." A minute later we were both in a hansom cab, driving furiously for the Brixton Road.

It was a foggy, cloudy morning, and a mist hung over the tops of the houses. My companion was in the best of spirits, and talked about violins, explaining the difference between a Stradivarius and an Amati. As for myself, I was silent, for the dull weather and the sad business depressed my spirits.

"You don't seem to give much thought to the matter in hand," I said at last, interrupting Holmes' musical discussion.

"No data yet," he answered. "It is a huge mistake to develop a theory before you have all the evidence. It biases the judgment."

"You will have your data soon," I remarked, pointing with my finger. "This is the Brixton Road, and that is the house, if I am not very much mistaken."

"So it is. Stop, driver, stop!" Holmes shouted.

We were still a hundred yards or so from it, but he insisted upon getting out and finishing our journey upon foot.

Number 3, Lauriston Gardens was one of four houses which stood back some little way from the street, two being occupied and two empty. A small garden lay in front of the houses, and across the garden was a narrow pathway made from a mixture of clay and gravel. The whole place was very sloppy from the rain that had fallen through the night. The garden was surrounded by a three foot tall brick wall, and against this wall a police officer was leaning, surrounded by a number of people hoping to get a glimpse of what was happening within.

I thought that Sherlock Holmes would run right into the house to learn the details of the mystery, but that was not his intention. Rather, he walked slowly up and down the pavement, and looked vacantly at the ground, the sky, the houses across the road, and the line of railings. He then went down the path, or rather down the grass next to the path, keeping his eyes upon the ground. Twice he stopped, and once I saw him smile. There were many footprints on the wet path, but since the police had been coming and going over it, I couldn't see how my companion could hope to learn anything from it.

At the door of the house we were met by a tall, white faced man, with a notebook in his hand, who rushed forward and wrung my companion's hand warmly. "It is indeed kind of you to come," he said. "I have had everything left untouched."

"Except that!" my friend answered, pointing at the pathway. "If a herd of buffaloes had passed along there could not be a greater mess. No doubt, however, you had drawn your own conclusions, Gregson, before you allowed this."

"I have had so much to do inside the house," the detective said evasively. "My colleague, Mr. Lestrade, is here. I had relied upon him to look after this."

Holmes glanced at me and raised his eyebrows. "With two such men as yourself and Lestrade upon the ground, there will not be much for me to find out," he said.

Gregson rubbed his hands in a self-satisfied way. "I think we have done all that can be done," he answered. "It's a queer case though, and I know your taste for such things."

"You did not come here in a cab?" asked Sherlock Holmes.

"No, sir."

"Nor Lestrade?"

"No, sir."

"Then let us go and look at the room." He strode into the house, followed by Gregson.

A short dusty hallway led to the kitchen and offices. Two doors opened out of it to the left and to the right. One of these had obviously been closed for many weeks. The other belonged to the dining room, which was the room in which the mysterious affair had occurred. Holmes walked in, and I followed him with that quiet feeling in my heart which the presence of death inspires.

It was a large square room, looking even larger from the absence of furniture. Opposite the door was a fireplace, with a mantelpiece of imitation white marble.

On one corner of this was stuck the stump of a red wax candle. The only window was so dirty that the light coming through was hazy, and the entire apartment was coated in dust.

All these details I observed afterwards. At the time my attention was centered upon the single grim, motionless figure that lay stretched upon the floor, with vacant eyes staring up at the ceiling. It was that of a man about forty-three or forty-four years of age, middle sized, broad shouldered, with curly black hair, and a short stubbly beard. He was dressed in a heavy coat, light colored pants, and a new shirt. A top hat, well brushed and trim, was placed upon the floor beside him. His hands were clenched and his legs were interlocked as though his death had been a painful one. On his rigid face there stood an expression of horror, and as it seemed to me, of hatred, such as I have never seen upon a human. There was also something else, something more sinister, written upon the face, the type of features that only one who had done great evil in his life could have developed. I have seen death in many forms, but never has it appeared to me in a more fearsome aspect than in that dark, grimy apartment.

Lestrade, lean and ferret-like as ever, was standing by the doorway, and greeted my companion and myself.

"This case will make a stir, sir," he remarked. "It beats anything I have seen, and I am no chicken."

"There is no clue?" said Gregson.

"None at all," chimed in Lestrade.

Sherlock Holmes approached the body, and, kneeling down, examined it intently. "You are sure that there is no wound?" he asked, pointing to numerous splashes of blood which lay all round.

"Positive!" cried both detectives.

"Then, of course, this blood belongs to a second individual—presumably the murderer, if murder has been committed. It reminds me of the circumstances attendant on the death of Van Jansen, in Utrecht, in the year '34. Do you remember the case, Gregson?"

"No, sir."

"Read it up—you really should. There is nothing new under the sun. It has all been done before."

As he spoke, his nimble fingers were flying here, there, and everywhere, feeling, pressing, unbuttoning, examining, while his eyes wore the same far away expression which I have already remarked upon. So swiftly was the examination made, that one would hardly have guessed the minuteness with which it was conducted. Finally, he sniffed the dead man's lips, and then glanced at the soles of his patent leather boots.

"He has not been moved at all?" he asked.

"No more than was necessary for the purposes of our examination."

"You can take him to the mortuary now," he said. "There is nothing more to be learned."

Gregson had a stretcher and four men at hand. At his call they entered the room, and the stranger was lifted and carried out. As they raised him, a ring tinkled down and rolled across the floor. Lestrade grabbed it up and stared at it with mystified eyes.

"There's been a woman here," he cried. "It's a woman's wedding ring."

He held it out, as he spoke, upon the palm of

his hand. We all gathered round him and gazed at it. There could be no doubt that that circlet of plain gold had once adorned the finger of a bride.

"This complicates matters," said Gregson. "Heaven knows, they were complicated enough before."

"You're sure it doesn't simplify them?" observed Holmes. "There's nothing to be learned by staring at it. What did you find in his pockets?"

"We have it all here," said Gregson, pointing to a pile of objects upon the bottom step of the stairs. "A gold watch, No. 97163, by Barraud, of London. Gold chain, very heavy and solid. Gold ring, with masonic symbol. Gold pin—bulldog's head, with rubies as eyes. Russian leather card case, with cards of Enoch J. Drebber of Cleveland, corresponding with the E. J. D. upon his jacket. No wallet, but loose money totaling seven pounds thirteen. Pocket edition of Boccaccio's 'Decameron,' with name of Joseph Stangerson upon the inside cover. Two letters—one addressed to E. J. Drebber and one to Joseph Stangerson."

"At what address?"

"American Exchange, Strand—to be left until called for. They are both from the Guion Steamship Company, and refer to the sailing of their boats from Liverpool. It is clear that this unfortunate man was about to return to New York."

"Have you made any inquiries as to this man, Stangerson?"

"I did it at once, sir," said Gregson. "I have had advertisements sent to all the newspapers, and one of my men has gone to the American Exchange, but he has not returned yet."

"Have you sent to Cleveland?"

"We telegraphed this morning."

"How did you word your inquiries?"

"We simply detailed the circumstances, and said that we should be glad of any information which could help us."

"You did not ask for particulars on any point which appeared to you to be crucial?"

"I asked about that other guy, Stangerson."

"Nothing else? Is there no circumstance on which this whole case appears to hinge? Will you not telegraph again?"

"I have said all I have to say," said Gregson, in an offended voice.

Sherlock Holmes chuckled to himself, and appeared to be about to make some remark, when Lestrade, who had been in the front room while we were holding this conversation in the hall, reappeared upon the scene, rubbing his hands in a pompous and self-satisfied manner.

"Mr. Gregson," he said, "I have just made a discovery of the highest importance, and one which would have been overlooked had I not made a careful examination of the walls."

The little man's eyes sparkled as he spoke, and he was evidently in a state of suppressed exultation at having scored a point against his colleague.

"Come here," Lestrade commanded, bustling back into the room, the atmosphere of which felt clearer since the removal of its ghastly inmate. "Now, stand there!"

He struck a match on his boot and held it up against the wall.

"Look at that!" he said, triumphantly.

The wallpaper had fallen away in parts of the house, and in this particular corner of the room a large piece had peeled off, leaving a yellow square of coarse plastering. Across this bare space there was scrawled in blood-red letters a single word—

RACHE

"What do you think of that?" cried the detective, with the air of a showman exhibiting his show. "This was overlooked because it was in the darkest corner of the room, and no one thought of looking there. The murderer has written it with his or her own blood. See this smear where it has trickled down the wall! That disposes of the idea of suicide anyhow. Why was that corner chosen to write it on? I will tell you. See that candle on the mantelpiece. It was lit at the time, and when it was lit this corner would be the brightest instead of the darkest portion of the wall."

"And what does it mean now that you have found it?" asked Gregson.

"Mean? Why, it means that the writer was going to put the female name Rachel, but was disturbed before he or she had time to finish. You mark my words, when this case comes to be cleared up you will find that a woman named Rachel has something to do with it. It's all very well for you to laugh, Mr. Sherlock Holmes. You may be very smart and clever, but the old hound is the best, when all is said and done."

"I really beg your pardon!" said my companion, who had ruffled the little man's temper by bursting into an explosion of laughter. "You certainly have the credit of being the first of us to find this out, and, as you say, it bears every mark of having been written by the other participant in last night's mystery. I have not had time to examine this room yet, but with your permission I shall do so now."

As he spoke, he whipped a tape measure and a large round magnifying glass from his pocket. With these two implements he trotted noiselessly about the room, sometimes stopping, occasionally kneeling, and once lying flat upon his face. So engrossed was he with his occupation that he appeared to have forgotten our presence, for he chattered away to himself under his breath the whole time, keeping up a running fire of exclamations, groans, whistles, and little cries suggestive of encouragement and of hope.

As I watched him I was irresistibly reminded of a pure blooded, well trained foxhound as it dashes backwards and forwards through the bushes, whining in its eagerness, until it comes across the lost scent. For twenty minutes or more he continued his researches, measuring with the most exact care the distance between marks which were entirely invisible to me, and occasionally applying his tape to the walls in an equally incomprehensible manner. In one place he gathered up very carefully a little pile of grey dust from the floor, and packed it away in an envelope. Finally, he examined with his glass the word upon the wall, going over every letter of it with the most minute exactness. This done, he appeared to be satisfied, for he replaced his tape and his glass in his pocket.

"They say that genius is an infinite capacity for taking pains," he remarked with a smile. "It's a very bad definition, but it does apply to detective work."

Gregson and Lestrade had watched the maneuvers of their amateur companion with considerable curiosity and some contempt. They evidently failed to appreciate the fact, which I had begun to realize, that Sherlock Holmes' smallest actions were all directed towards some definite and practical end.

"What do you think of it, sir?" they both asked.

"It would be robbing you both of the credit for the case if I was to presume to help you," remarked my friend. "You are doing so well now that it would be a pity for anyone to interfere." There was a world of sarcasm in his voice as he spoke. "If you will let me know how your investigations go," he continued, "I shall be happy to give you any help I can. In the meantime I should like to speak to the constable who found the body. Can you give me his name and address?"

Lestrade glanced at his notebook. "John Rance," he said. "He is off duty now. You will find him at 46, Audley Court, Kennington Park Gate."

Holmes took a note of the address.

"Come along, Doctor," he said; "we shall go and look him up. I'll tell you one thing which may help you in the case," he continued, turning to the two detectives. "There has been murder done, and the murderer was a man. He was more than six feet high, was in the prime of life, had small feet for his height, wore coarse, square toed boots and smoked a Trichinopoly cigar. He came here with his victim in a four wheeled cab, which was drawn by a horse with three old shoes and one new one on his front left leg. In all probability the murderer had a ruddy face, and the fingernails of his right hand were remarkably long. These are only a few indications, but they may assist you."

Lestrade and Gregson glanced at each other with an incredulous smile.

"If this man was murdered, how was it done?" asked the former.

"Poison," said Sherlock Holmes curtly, and strode off. "One other thing, Lestrade," he added, turning round at the door: "'Rache,' is the German for 'revenge;' so don't lose your time looking for Miss Rachel."

With which he walked away, leaving the two rivals open mouthed behind him.

CHAPTER IV.
WHAT JOHN RANCE HAD TO TELL

IT was one o'clock when we left No. 3, Lauriston Gardens. Sherlock Holmes led me to the nearest telegraph office, from where he dispatched a long telegram. He then hailed a cab, and ordered the driver to take us to the address given us by Lestrade.

"There is nothing like first hand evidence," he remarked. "As a matter of fact, my mind is entirely made up upon the case, but still we may as well learn all that is to be learned."

"You amaze me, Holmes," said I. "Surely you are not as sure as you pretend to be of all those particulars which you gave?"

"There's no room for a mistake," he answered. "The very first thing which I observed on arriving there was that a cab had made two ruts with its wheels close to the curb. Now, up to last night, we have had no rain for a week, so those wheels which left such a deep impression must have been there during the night. There were the marks of the horse's hoofs, too, the outline of one of which was far more clearly cut than that of the other three, showing that that was a new shoe. Since the cab was there after the rain began, and was not there at any time during the morning—I have Gregson's word for that—it follows that it must have been there during the night, and, therefore, that it brought those two individuals to the house."

"That seems simple enough," said I. "But how about the other man's height?"

"Why, the height of a man, in nine cases out of ten, can be told from the length of his stride. It is a simple enough calculation, though there is no use my boring you with figures. I had this fellow's stride both on the clay outside and on the dust within. Then I had a way of checking my calculation. When a man writes on a wall, his instinct leads him to write about the level of his own eyes. Now that writing was just over six feet from the ground. It was child's play."

"And his age?" I asked.

"Well, if a man can stride four and a half feet without the smallest effort, he can't be too old and feeble. That was the breadth of a puddle on the garden walk which he had evidently walked across. Patent leather boots had gone round, and Square toes had hopped over. There is no mystery about it at all. I am simply applying to ordinary life a few of those rules of observation and deduction which I advocated in that article. Is there anything else that puzzles you?"

"The finger nails and the Trichinopoly cigar," I suggested.

"The writing on the wall was done with a man's forefinger dipped in blood. My magnifying glass allowed me to observe that the plaster was slightly scratched in doing it, which would not have been the case if the man's nail had been trimmed. I gathered up some scattered ash from the floor. It was dark in color and flakey—such an ash as is only made by a Trichinopoly. I have made a special study of cigar ashes—in fact, I have written a monograph upon the subject. I flatter myself that I can distinguish at a glance the ash of any known brand, either of cigar or of tobacco. It is just in such details that the skilled detective differs from the Gregson and Lestrade type."

"And the ruddy face?" I asked.

"Ah, that was a more daring shot, though I have no doubt that I was right. You must not ask me that at the moment."

I passed my hand over my brow. "My head is in a whirl," I remarked; "the more one thinks of it the more mysterious it grows. How came these two men—if there were two men—into an empty house? What has become of the cabman who drove them? How could one man compel another to take poison? Where did the blood come from? What was the objective of the murderer, since robbery had no part in it? How came the woman's ring to be there? Above all, why should the second man write up the German word RACHE before leaving? I confess that I cannot see any possible way of reconciling all these facts."

My companion smiled approvingly. "You sum up the difficulties of the situation succinctly and well," he said. "There is much that is still obscure, though I have quite made up my mind on the main facts. As to poor Lestrade's discovery it was simply a blind intended to put the police upon a wrong track, by suggesting Socialism and secret societies. It was not done by a German. The A, if you noticed, was printed somewhat after the German fashion. Now, a real German invariably prints in the Latin character, so that we may safely say that this was not written by a German, but by a clumsy imitator who overdid his part. It was simply a ruse to divert questions in the wrong direction. I'm not going to tell you much more of the case, Doctor. You know a magician gets no credit when once he has explained his tricks, and if I show you too much of my method of working, you will come to the conclusion that I am a very ordinary individual after all."

"I shall never do that," I answered. "You have brought detection as near to an exact science as it ever will be brought in this world."

My companion flushed up with pleasure at my words, and the earnest way in which I uttered them. I had already observed that he was sensitive to flattery regarding his art.

"I'll tell you one other thing," he said. "Patent leathers and Square toes came in the same cab, and they walked down the pathway together as friendly as possible—arm-in-arm, in all probability. When they got inside they walked up and down the room—or rather, Patent leathers stood still while Square toes walked up and down. I could read all that in the dust; and I could read that as he walked he grew more and more excited. That is shown by the increased length of his strides. He was talking all the while, and working himself up, no doubt, into a fury. Then the tragedy occurred. I've told you all I know myself now, for the rest is mere conjecture. We have a good working basis, however, on which to start. We must hurry up, for I want to go to Halle's concert hall to hear Norman Neruda this afternoon."

This conversation had occurred while our cab

had been threading its way through a long succession of dingy streets and dreary alleys. In the most dingy and dreary of them our driver suddenly came to a stand. "That's Audley Court in there," he said, pointing to a narrow slit in the line of brick. "You'll find me here when you come back."

Audley Court was not an attractive place. We picked our way among groups of dirty children and lines of hanging laundry until we came to Number 46. On asking, we found that the constable was in bed, and we were shown into a little front parlor to wait for him.

He appeared looking a little irritable at being disturbed in his sleep. "I made my report at the office," he said.

Holmes took a half-pound coin from his pocket and flipped it over in his fingers. "We thought that we should like to hear it all from your own lips," he said.

"I shall be most happy to tell you anything I can," the constable answered with his eyes upon the little golden coin.

"Just let us hear it all in your own way as it occurred."

Rance sat down on the horsehair sofa, and knitted his brows as though determined not to omit anything in his story.

"I'll tell it ye from the beginning," he said. "My time is from ten at night to six in the morning. At eleven there was a fight at the 'White Hart'; but besides that all was quiet enough on the beat. At one o'clock it began to rain, and I met Harry Murcher—him who has the Holland Grove beat—and we stood together at the corner of Henrietta Street a-talkin'. Presently—maybe about two or a little after—I thought I would take a look round and see that all was right down the Brixton Road. It was precious dirty and lonely. Not a soul did I meet all the way down, though a cab or two went past me. I was a strollin' down, thinkin' between ourselves how uncommon handy a drink would be, when suddenly the glint of a light caught my eye in the window of that same house. Now, I knew that them two houses in Lauriston Gardens was empty, on account of him that owns them who won't have the drains fixed, which caused the very last tenant what lived in one of them to die o' typhoid fever. I was knocked all in a heap therefore at seeing a light in the window, and I suspected as something was wrong. When I got to the door—"

"You stopped, and then walked back to the garden gate," my companion interrupted. "What did you do that for?"

Rance gave a violent jump, and stared at Sherlock Holmes with the utmost amazement upon his features.

"Why, that's true, sir," he said; "though how you come to know it, Heaven only knows. Ye see, when I got up to the door it was so still and so lonesome, that I thought I'd be none the worse for some one with me. I ain't afeared of anything on this side o' the grave; but I thought that maybe it was him that died o' the typhoid inspecting the drains what killed him. The thought gave me a kind o' turn, and I walked back to the gate to see if I could see Murcher's lantern, but there wasn't no sign of him nor of anyone else."

"There was no one in the street?"

"Not a livin' soul, sir, nor so much as a dog.

Then I pulled myself together and went back and pushed the door open. All was quiet inside, so I went into the room where the light was a-burnin'. There was a candle flickerin' on the mantelpiece—a red wax one—and by its light I saw—"

"Yes, I know all that you saw. You walked round the room several times, and you knelt down by the body, and then you walked through and tried the kitchen door, and then—"

John Rance sprang to his feet with a frightened face and suspicion in his eyes. "Where was you hid to see all that?" he cried. "It seems to me that you knows a deal more than you should."

Holmes laughed and threw his card across the table to the constable. "Don't go arresting me for the murder," he said. "I am one of the hounds, not the wolf; Mr. Gregson or Mr. Lestrade will answer for that. Go on, though. What did you do next?"

Rance resumed his seat, without losing his mystified expression. "I went back to the gate and sounded my whistle. That brought Murcher and two more to the spot."

"Was the street empty then?"

"Well, it was, as far as anybody that could be of any good goes."

"What do you mean?"

The constable's features broadened into a grin. "I've seen many a drunk chap in my time," he said, "but never anyone so cryin' drunk as that chap. He was at the gate when I came out, a-leanin' up agin the railings, and a-singin' at the pitch o' his lungs about Columbine's Newfangled Banner, or some such stuff. He couldn't stand, far less help."

"What sort of a man was he?" asked Sherlock Holmes.

John Rance appeared to be somewhat irritated at this digression. "He was an uncommon drunk sort o' man," he said. "He'd have found himself in the station if we hadn't been so busy."

"His face—his dress—didn't you notice them?" Holmes broke in impatiently.

"I should think I did notice them, seeing that I had to prop him up—me and Murcher between us. He was a long chap, with a red face, the lower part muffled round—"

"That will do," cried Holmes. "What became of him?"

"We'd enough to do without lookin' after him," the policeman said, in an aggrieved voice. "I'll wager he found his way home all right."

"How was he dressed?"

"A brown overcoat."

"Had he a whip in his hand?"

"A whip—no."

"He must have left it behind," muttered my companion. "You didn't happen to see or hear a cab after that?"

"No."

"There's a half-sovereign for you," my companion said, standing up and taking his hat. "I am afraid, Rance, that you will never rise in the force. That head of yours should be for thinking as well as decoration. You might have gained your sergeant's stripes last night. The man whom you held in your hands is the man who holds the clue of this mystery, and whom we are seeking. There is no use of arguing about it now; I tell you that it is so. Come along, Doctor."

We started off for the cab together, leaving our informant incredulous, but obviously uncomfortable.

"The blundering fool," Holmes said, bitterly, as we drove back to our lodgings. "Just to think of his having such an incomparable bit of good luck, and not taking advantage of it."

"I am rather in the dark still," I broke in. "It is true that the description of this man tallies with your idea of the second party in this mystery. But why should he come back to the house after leaving it? That is not the way of criminals."

"The ring, man, the ring: that was what he came back for. If we have no other way of catching him, we can always bait our line with the ring. I shall have him, Doctor—I'll lay you two to one that I have him. I must thank you for it all. I might not have gone but for you, and so would have missed the finest study I ever came across: a study in scarlet, eh? Why shouldn't we use a little art jargon? There's the scarlet thread of murder running through the colorless coil of life, and our duty is to unravel it, and isolate it, and expose every inch of it. And now for lunch, and then for Norman Neruda. Her attack and her bowing are splendid. What's that little thing of Chopin's she plays so magnificently? Tra-la-la-lira-lira-lay."

Leaning back in the cab, this amateur bloodhound sang away like a lark while I meditated upon the many sidedness of the human mind.

CHAPTER V.
OUR ADVERTISEMENT BRINGS A VISITOR

OUR morning's exertions had been too much for my weak health, and I was tired out in the afternoon. After Holmes' departure for the concert, I lay down upon the sofa and tried to get a couple of hours' sleep. It was a useless attempt. My mind had been too much excited by all that had occurred. Every time that I closed my eyes I saw before me the twisted face of the murdered man. So sinister was the impression which that face had produced upon me that I found it difficult to feel anything but gratitude for the man who had removed its owner from the world. If ever human features indicated its owner was full of vice, they were certainly those of Enoch J. Drebber, of Cleveland. Still I recognized that justice must be done, and that the depravity of the victim did not condone murder in the eyes of the law.

The more I thought of it, the more extraordinary my companion's hypothesis that the man had been poisoned, appeared. I remembered how he had sniffed his lips, and had no doubt that he had detected something which had given rise to the idea.

Then, again, if not poison, what had caused the man's death, since there was neither wound nor marks of strangulation? But, on the other hand, whose blood was that on the wall? There were no signs of a struggle, nor had the victim any weapon with which he might have wounded an antagonist. As long as all these questions were unsolved, I felt that sleep would be no easy matter, either for Holmes or myself. His quiet self-confident manner convinced me that he had already formed a theory which explained all the facts, though what it was I could not guess.

He was very late in returning—so late, that I knew that the concert could not have detained him all the time. Dinner was on the table before he appeared.

"It was magnificent," he said, as he took his seat. "Do you remember what Darwin says about music? He claims that the power of producing and appreciating it existed among the human race long before the power of speech was arrived at. Perhaps that is why we are so subtly influenced by it. There are vague memories in our souls of those misty centuries when the world was in its childhood."

"That's rather a broad idea," I remarked.

"One's ideas must be as broad as Nature if they are to interpret Nature," he answered. "What's the matter? You're not looking quite yourself. This Brixton Road affair has upset you."

"To tell the truth, it has," I said. "I ought to be more case hardened after my Afghan experiences. I saw my own comrades hacked to pieces at Maiwand without losing my nerve."

"I can understand. There is a mystery about this which stimulates the imagination. Where there is no imagination there is no horror. Have you seen the evening paper?"

"No."

"It gives a fairly good account of the affair. It does not mention the fact that when the man was raised up, a woman's wedding ring fell upon the floor. It is just as well it does not."

"Why?"

"Look at this advertisement," he answered. "I had one sent to every paper this morning immediately after the affair."

He threw the paper across to me and I glanced at the place indicated. It was the first announcement in the "Found" column. "In Brixton Road, this morning," it ran, "a plain gold wedding ring, found in the roadway between the 'White Hart' Tavern and Holland Grove. Apply Dr. Watson, 221B, Baker Street, between eight and nine this evening."

"Excuse my using your name," he said. "If I used my own some of these dunderheads would recognize it, and want to meddle in the affair."

"That is all right," I answered. "But supposing anyone applies, I have no ring."

"Oh yes, you have," said he, handing me one. "This will do very well. It is almost a copy."

"And who do you expect will answer this advertisement."

"Why, the man in the brown coat—our ruddy friend with the square toes. If he does not come himself he will send an accomplice."

"Would he not consider it as too dangerous?"

"Not at all. If my view of the case is correct, and I have every reason to believe that it is, this man would rather risk anything than lose the ring. According to my notion he dropped it while stooping over Drebber's body, and did not miss it at the time. After leaving the house he discovered his loss and hurried back, but found the police already in possession, owing to his own folly in leaving the candle burning. He had to pretend to be drunk in order to allay the suspicions that might have been aroused by his appearance at the gate. Now put yourself in that man's place. On thinking the matter over, it must have occurred to him that it was possible that he had lost the ring in the road after leaving the house. What would he do, then? He would eagerly look out for the evening papers in the hope of seeing it among the articles found. His eye, of course, would find this. He would be overjoyed. Why should he fear a trap? There would be no reason in his eyes why the finding of the ring should be connected with the murder. He would come. He will come. You shall see him within an hour."

"And then?" I asked.

"Oh, you can leave me to deal with him then. Have you any arms?"

"I have my old service revolver and a few cartridges."

"You had better clean it and load it. He will be a desperate man, and though I shall take him unawares, it is just as well to be ready for anything."

I went to my bedroom and followed his advice. When I returned with the pistol the table had been cleared, and Holmes was engaged in his favorite occupation of playing his violin.

"The plot thickens," he said, as I entered. "I have just had an answer to my American telegram. My view of the case is the correct one."

"And that is?" I asked eagerly.

"My fiddle would be the better for new strings," he remarked. "Put your pistol in your pocket. When the fellow comes speak to him in an ordinary way. Leave the rest to me. Don't frighten him by looking at him too hard."

"It is eight o'clock now," I said, glancing at my watch.

"Yes. He will probably be here in a few minutes. Open the door slightly. That will do. Now put the key on the inside. Thank you! Here comes our man, I think."

As he spoke there was a sharp ring at the bell. Sherlock Holmes rose softly and moved his chair in the direction of the door. We heard the servant pass along the hall, and the sharp click of the latch as she opened it.

"Does Dr. Watson live here?" asked a clear but rather harsh voice. We could not hear the servant's reply, but the door closed, and someone began to ascend the stairs. The footfall was an uncertain and shuffling one. A look of surprise passed over the face of my companion as he listened to it. It came slowly along the passage, and there was a feeble tap at the door.

"Come in," I cried.

At my summons, instead of the man of violence whom we expected, a very old and wrinkled woman hobbled into the apartment. She appeared to be dazzled by the sudden blaze of light, and after dropping a curtsey, she stood blinking at us with her bleared eyes and fumbling in her pocket with nervous, shaky fingers. I glanced at my companion, and his face had assumed such an upset expression that it was all I could do to keep my countenance bland and neutral.

The old woman drew out an evening paper, and pointed at our advertisement. "It's this as has brought me, good gentlemen," she said, dropping another curtsey; "a gold wedding ring in the Brixton Road. It belongs to my girl Sally, as was married twelve months ago. Her husband is steward aboard a Union boat, and what he'd say if he come home and found her without her ring is more than I can think, he being short enough at the best o' times, but more especially when he has the drink. If it please you, she went to the circus last night along with—"

"Is that her ring?" I asked.

"The Lord be thanked!" cried the old woman; "Sally will be a glad woman this night. That's the ring."

"And what may your address be?" I inquired, taking up a pencil.

"13, Duncan Street, Houndsditch. A weary way from here."

"The Brixton Road does not lie between any circus and Houndsditch," said Sherlock Holmes sharply.

The old woman faced round and looked keenly at him from her little red rimmed eyes. "The gentleman asked me for *my* address," she said. "Sally lives in lodgings at 3, Mayfield Place, Peckham."

"And your name is—?"

"My name is Sawyer—her's is Dennis, which Tom Dennis married her—and a smart, clean lad, too, as long as he's at sea, and no steward in the company more thought of; but when on shore, what with the women and what with liquor shops—"

"Here is your ring, Mrs. Sawyer," I interrupted, in obedience to a sign from my companion; "it clearly belongs to your daughter, and I am glad to be able to restore it to the rightful owner."

With many mumbled blessings and protestations of gratitude the old woman packed it away in her pocket, and shuffled off down the stairs. Sherlock Holmes sprang to his feet the moment that she was gone and rushed into his room. He returned in a few seconds wearing his hat and jacket. "I'll follow her," he said, hurriedly; "she must be an accomplice, and will lead me to him. Wait up for me." The hall door had hardly slammed behind our visitor before Holmes had descended the stair. Looking through the window I could see her walking feebly along the other side, while her pursuer dogged her some little distance behind. "Either his whole theory is incorrect," I thought to myself, "or else he will be led now to the heart of the mystery." There was no need for him to ask me to wait up for him, for I felt that sleep was impossible until I heard the result of his adventure.

It was close upon nine when he set out. I had no idea how long he might be, but I sat puffing at my pipe and skipping over the pages of Henri Murger's "Vie de Bohème." Ten o'clock passed, and I heard the footsteps of the maid as she pattered off to bed. Eleven, and the more stately tread of the landlady passed my door, bound for the same destination. It was close upon twelve before I heard the sharp sound of his latch key. The instant he entered I saw by his face that he had not been successful. Amusement and chagrin seemed to be struggling for the mastery, until the former suddenly carried the day, and he burst into a hearty laugh.

"I wouldn't have the Scotland Yarders know it for the world," he cried, dropping into his chair; "I have mocked them so much that they would never have let me hear the end of it. I can afford to laugh, because I know that I will be even with them in the long run."

"What is it then?" I asked.

"Oh, I don't mind telling a story against myself. That creature had gone a little way when she began to limp and show every sign of being foot sore. Presently she came to a halt, and hailed a passing cab. I managed to be close to her so as to hear the address, but I need not have been so anxious, for she sang it out loud enough to be heard at the other side of the street, 'Drive to 13, Duncan Street, Houndsditch,' she cried. This begins to look genuine, I thought, and having seen her safely inside, I perched myself behind. That's an art which every detective should be an expert at. Well, away we rattled, and never slowed until we reached the street in question. I hopped off before we came to the door, and strolled down the street in an easy, lounging way. I saw the cab pull up. The driver jumped down, and I saw him open the door and stand expectantly. Nothing came out, though. When I reached him he was groping about frantically in the empty cab, and giving vent to the finest assorted collection of oaths that ever I listened to. There was no sign or trace of his passenger, and I fear it will be some time before he gets his fare. On inquiring at Number 13 we found that the house belonged to a respectable paperhanger named Keswick, and that no one of the name either of Sawyer or Dennis had ever been heard of there."

"You don't mean to say," I cried, in amazement, "that that tottering, feeble old woman was able to get out of the cab while it was in motion, without either you or the driver seeing her?"

"Hardly an old woman!" said Sherlock Holmes, sharply. "We were the old women to be so taken in. It must have been a young man, and an active one, too, besides being an incomparable actor. The get up was inimitable. He saw that he was followed, no doubt, and used this means of giving me the slip. It shows that the man we are after is not as lonely as I imagined he was, but has friends who are ready to risk something for him. Now, Doctor, you are looking done up. Take my advice and turn in."

I was certainly feeling very weary, so I obeyed his instructions. I left Holmes seated in front of the smoldering fire, and long into the watches of the night I heard the low, melancholy wailings of his violin, and knew that he was still pondering over the strange problem which he had set himself to unravel.

CHAPTER VI.
TOBIAS GREGSON SHOWS WHAT HE CAN DO

THE papers next day were full of the "Brixton Mystery," as they termed it. Each had a long account of the affair, and many had it as the top headline of the day. There was some information in them which was new to me. Here is a condensation of a few of them:

The *Daily Telegraph* remarked that in the history of crime there had seldom been a tragedy which presented stranger features. The German name of the victim, the absence of all other motive, and the sinister inscription on the wall, all pointed to its being done by political refugees and revolutionists. The Socialists had many branches in America, and the deceased had, no doubt, infringed their unwritten laws, and been tracked down by them. The article concluded by advising the Government to keep a closer watch over foreigners in England.

The *Standard* commented upon the fact that lawless outrages of the sort usually occurred under a Liberal Administration. They arose from the unsettling of the minds of the masses, and the consequent weakening of all authority. The deceased was an

American gentleman who had been residing for some weeks in London. He had stayed at the boarding house of Madame Charpentier, in Torquay Terrace, Camberwell. He was accompanied in his travels by his private secretary, Mr. Joseph Stangerson. The two bade goodbye to their landlady that afternoon and departed to Euston Station with the intention of catching the Liverpool express. They were afterwards seen together upon the platform. Nothing more is known of them until Mr. Drebber's body was, as recorded, discovered in an empty house in the Brixton Road, many miles from Euston. How he came there, or how he met his fate, are questions which are still involved in mystery. Nothing is known of the whereabouts of Stangerson. We are glad to learn that Mr. Lestrade and Mr. Gregson, of Scotland Yard, are both engaged upon the case, and it is confidently anticipated that these well known officers will speedily throw light upon the matter.

The *Daily News* observed that there was no doubt as to the crime being a political one. The hatred of Liberalism in other European governments had the effect of driving to our shores a number of men who might have otherwise made excellent citizens were they not soured by the memories of all that they had undergone. Among these men there was a stringent code of honor, any infringement of which was punished by death. Every effort should be made to find the secretary, Stangerson, and to ascertain details of the habits of the deceased. A great step had been gained by the discovery of the address of the house at which he had boarded—a result which was entirely due to the acuteness and energy of Mr. Gregson of Scotland Yard.

Sherlock Holmes and I read these notices over together at breakfast, and they appeared to afford him considerable amusement.

"I told you that, whatever happened, Lestrade and Gregson would be sure to score."

"That depends on how it turns out."

"Oh, bless you, it doesn't matter in the least. If the man is caught, it will be *on account* of their exertions; if he escapes, it will be *in spite* of their exertions. It's heads I win and tails you lose. Whatever they do, they will have followers."

"What on earth is this?" I cried, for at this moment there came the pattering of many steps in the hall and on the stairs, accompanied by loud expressions of disgust upon the part of our landlady.

"It's the Baker Street division of the detective police force," said my companion, and as he spoke there rushed into the room half a dozen of the dirtiest and most ragged street kids that ever I clapped eyes on.

"Attention!" cried Holmes, in a sharp tone, and the six dirty little scoundrels stood in a line like so many statues. "In future you shall send up Wiggins alone to report, and the rest of you must wait in the street. Have you found it, Wiggins?"

"No, sir, we hain't," said one of the youths.

"I hardly expected you would. You must keep on until you do. Here are your wages." He handed each of them a shilling.

"Now, off you go, and come back with a better report next time."

He waved his hand, and they scampered away downstairs like so many rats, and we heard their shrill voices next moment in the street.

"There's more work to be got out of one of those little beggars than out of a dozen of the force," Holmes remarked. "The mere sight of an official looking person seals men's lips. These youngsters, however, go everywhere and hear everything. They are as sharp as needles, too; all they want is organization."

"Is it on this Brixton case that you are employing them?" I asked.

"Yes; there is a point which I wish to know. It is merely a matter of time. Hullo! we are going to hear some news now with a vengeance! Here is Gregson coming down the road with a smile written upon every feature of his face. Bound for us, I know. Yes, he is stopping. There he is!"

There was a violent ring at the bell, and in a few seconds the fair haired detective came up the stairs, three steps at a time, and burst into our sitting room.

"My dear fellow," he cried, wringing Holmes' unresponsive hand, "congratulate me! I have made the whole thing as clear as day."

A shade of anxiety seemed to me to cross my companion's expressive face. "Do you mean that you are on the right track?" he asked.

"The right track! Why, sir, we have the man under lock and key."

"And his name is?"

"Arthur Charpentier, sub-lieutenant in Her Majesty's navy," cried Gregson, rubbing his fat hands and inflating his chest.

Sherlock Holmes gave a sigh of relief, and relaxed into a smile.

"Take a seat, and try one of these cigars," he

said. "We are anxious to know how you managed it. Will you have some whiskey and water?"

"I don't mind if I do," the detective answered. "The tremendous efforts which I have gone through during the last day or two have worn me out. Not so much bodily effort, you understand, as the strain upon the mind. You will appreciate that, Mr. Sherlock Holmes, for we are both brain workers."

"You do me too much honor," said Holmes, gravely. "Let us hear how you arrived at this most gratifying result."

The detective seated himself in the arm chair and puffed at his cigar. Then suddenly he slapped his thigh in amusement.

"The fun of it is," he cried, "that that fool Lestrade, who thinks himself so smart, has gone off upon the wrong track altogether. He is after the secretary Stangerson, who had no more to do with the crime than an unborn baby. I have no doubt that he has caught him by this time." The idea tickled Gregson so much that he laughed until he choked.

"And how did you get your clue?"

"Ah, I'll tell you all about it. Of course, Doctor Watson, this is strictly between ourselves. The first difficulty we encountered was finding where this American had been. Some people would have waited until their advertisements were answered, or until parties came forward and volunteered information. That is not Tobias Gregson's way of going to work. You remember the hat beside the dead man?"

"Yes," said Holmes; "by John Underwood and Sons, 129, Camberwell Road."

Gregson looked quite crestfallen. "I had no idea

that you noticed that," he said. "Have you been there?"

"No."

"Ha!" cried Gregson, in a relieved voice, "you should never neglect a chance, however small it may seem."

"To a great mind, nothing is little," remarked Holmes.

"Well, I went to Underwood, and asked him if he had sold a hat of that size and description. He looked over his books, and came on it at once. He had sent the hat to a Mr. Drebber, residing at Charpentier's Boarding Establishment, Torquay Terrace. Thus I got at his address."

"Smart—very smart!" murmured Sherlock Holmes.

"I next called upon Madame Charpentier," continued the detective. "I found her very pale and upset. Her daughter was in the room, too—an uncommonly fine girl she is—she was looking red about the eyes and her lips trembled as I spoke to her. That didn't escape my notice. I began to smell a rat. You know the feeling, Mr. Sherlock Holmes, when you come upon the right scent—a kind of thrill in your nerves. 'Have you heard of the mysterious death of your late boarder Mr. Enoch J. Drebber, of Cleveland?' I asked.

"The mother nodded. She didn't seem able to get out a word. The daughter burst into tears. I felt more than ever that these people knew something of the matter.

"'At what time did Mr. Drebber leave your house for the train?' I asked.

"'At eight o'clock,' she said, gulping in her

throat to keep down her agitation. 'His secretary, Mr. Stangerson, said that there were two trains—one at 9.15 and one at 11. He was hoping to catch the first.

"'And was that the last which you saw of him?'

"A terrible change came over the woman's face as I asked the question. Her features turned perfectly livid. It was some seconds before she could get out the single word 'Yes'—and when it did come it was in a husky unnatural tone.

"There was silence for a moment, and then the daughter spoke in a calm clear voice.

"'No good can ever come of falsehood, mother,' she said. 'Let us be frank with this gentleman. We *did* see Mr. Drebber again.'

"'God forgive you!' cried Madame Charpentier, throwing up her hands and sinking back in her chair. 'You have murdered your brother.'

"'Arthur would rather that we spoke the truth,' the girl answered firmly.

"'You had best tell me all about it now,' I said. 'Half-confidences are worse than none. Besides, you do not know how much we know of it.'

"'On your head be it, Alice!' cried her mother; and then, turning to me, 'I will tell you all, sir. Do not imagine that my agitation on behalf of my son arises from any fear lest he should have had a hand in this terrible affair. He is utterly innocent of it. My dread is, however, that in your eyes and in the eyes of others he may appear to be compromised. That however is surely impossible. His high character and his profession would all forbid it.'

"'Your best way is to make a clean admission of the facts,' I answered. 'Depend upon it that if your son is innocent he will be none the worse.'

"'Perhaps, Alice, you had better leave us together,' she said, and her daughter left. 'Now, sir,' she continued, 'I had no intention of telling you all this, but since my poor daughter has disclosed it I have no alternative. Having once decided to speak, I will tell you all without omitting any particular.'

"'It is your wisest course,' said I.

"'Mr. Drebber has been with us nearly three weeks. He and his secretary, Mr. Stangerson, had been traveling on the Continent. I noticed a "Copenhagen" label upon each of their trunks, showing that that had been their last stopping place. Stangerson was a quiet reserved man, but his employer, I am sorry to say, was far otherwise. He was coarse in his habits and brutish in his ways. The very night of his arrival he became very much the worse for drink, and, indeed, after twelve o'clock in the day he could hardly ever be said to be sober. His manners towards the maid servants were disgustingly free and familiar. Worst of all, he speedily assumed the same attitude towards my daughter, Alice, and spoke to her more than once in a way which, fortunately, she is too innocent to understand. On one occasion he actually seized her in his arms and embraced her—an outrage which caused his own secretary to reproach him for his unmanly conduct.'

"'But why did you stand all this?' I asked. 'I suppose that you can get rid of your boarders when you wish.'

"Mrs. Charpentier blushed at my pertinent question. 'Would to God that I had given him notice on the very day that he came,' she said. 'But they were paying a pound a day each—fourteen pounds a week, and this is the quiet season. I am a widow, and my boy in the Navy has cost me much. I didn't want to lose the money. I acted for the best. This last was too much, however, and I told him to leave because of it. That was the reason of his going.'

"'Well?'

"'My heart grew light when I saw him drive away. My son is on leave just now, but I did not tell him anything of all this, for his temper is violent, and he is very fond of his sister. When I closed the door behind them a load seemed to be lifted from my mind. Alas, in less than an hour there was a ring at the bell, and I learned that Mr. Drebber had returned. He was much excited and clearly drunk. He forced his way into the room, where I was sitting with my daughter, and said he missed his train. He then turned to Alice, and before my very face, proposed to her that she should run away with him. "You are of age," he said, "and there is no law to stop you. I have money enough and to spare. Never mind your old mother here, but come along with me now straight away. You shall live like a princess." Poor Alice was so frightened that she shrunk away from him, but he caught her by the wrist and tried to drag her towards the door. I screamed, and at that moment my son Arthur came into the room. What happened then I do not know. I heard oaths and the confused sounds of a fight. I was too terrified to raise my head. When I did look up I saw Arthur standing in the doorway laughing, with a stick in his hand. "I don't think that fine fellow will trouble us again," he said. "I will just go after him and see what he does with himself." With those words he took his hat and started off down the street. The next morning we heard of Mr. Drebber's mysterious death.'

"This statement came from Mrs. Charpentier's lips with many gasps and pauses. At times she spoke so low that I could hardly catch the words. I made shorthand notes of all that she said, however, so that there should be no possibility of a mistake."

"It's quite exciting," said Sherlock Holmes, with a yawn. "What happened next?"

"When Mrs. Charpentier paused," the detective continued, "I saw that the whole case hung upon one point. Fixing her with my eye in a way which I always found effective with women, I asked her at what hour her son returned.

"'I do not know,' she answered.

"'Not know?'

"'No; he has a key, and he let himself in.'

"'After you went to bed?'

"'Yes.'

"'When did you go to bed?'

"'About eleven.'

"'So your son was gone at least two hours?'

"'Yes.'

"'Possibly four or five?'

"'Yes.'

"'What was he doing during that time?'

"'I do not know,' she answered, turning white to her very lips.

"Of course after that there was nothing more to be done. I found out where Lieutenant Charpentier was, took two officers with me, and arrested him. When I touched him on the shoulder and warned him to come quietly with us, he answered us as bold as brass, 'I suppose you are arresting me for being concerned in the death of that scoundrel Drebber,' he said. We had said nothing to him about it, so his alluding to it had a most suspicious aspect."

"Very," said Holmes.

"He still carried the heavy stick which the mother described him as having with him when he followed Drebber. It was a stout oak cudgel."

"What is your theory, then?"

"Well, my theory is that he followed Drebber as far as the Brixton Road. When there, a fresh fight arose between them, in the course of which Drebber received a blow from the stick, in the pit of the stomach, perhaps, which killed him without leaving any mark. The night was so wet that no one was about, so Charpentier dragged the body of his victim into the empty house. As to the candle, and the blood, and the writing on the wall, and the ring, they may all be so many tricks to throw the police on to the wrong scent."

"Well done!" said Holmes in an encouraging voice. "Really, Gregson, you are getting along. We shall make something of you yet."

"I flatter myself that I have managed it rather neatly," the detective answered proudly. "The young man volunteered a statement, in which he said that after following Drebber some time, the latter perceived him, and took a cab in order to get away from him. On his way home he met an old shipmate, and took a long walk with him. On being asked where this old shipmate lived, he was unable to give any satisfactory reply. I think the whole case fits together uncommonly well. What amuses me is to think of Lestrade, who had started off upon the wrong scent. I am afraid he won't make much of— Why, by Jove, here's the very man himself!"

It was indeed Lestrade, who had ascended the stairs while we were talking, and who now entered the room. His face was disturbed and troubled, while his clothes were disarranged and untidy. He had evidently come with the intention of consulting with Sherlock Holmes, for on perceiving his colleague he appeared to be embarrassed and put out. He stood in the centre of the room, fumbling nervously with his hat and uncertain what to do. "This is a most extraordinary case," he said at last—"a most incomprehensible affair."

"Ah, you find it so, Mr. Lestrade!" cried Gregson, triumphantly. "I thought you would come to that conclusion. Have you managed to find the secretary, Mr. Joseph Stangerson?"

"The secretary, Mr. Joseph Stangerson," said Lestrade gravely, "was murdered at Halliday's Private Hotel about six o'clock this morning."

CHAPTER VII.
LIGHT IN THE DARKNESS

THE information with which Lestrade greeted us was so momentous and so unexpected, that we were all three fairly dumfounded. Gregson sprang out of his chair and knocked over the remainder of his whiskey and water. I stared in silence at Sherlock Holmes, whose lips were compressed. "Stangerson too!" he muttered. "The plot thickens."

"It was quite thick enough before," grumbled Lestrade, taking a chair. "I seem to have dropped into a sort of council of war."

"Are you—are you sure of this piece of intelligence?" stammered Gregson.

"I have just come from his room," said Lestrade. "I was the first to discover what had occurred."

"We have been hearing Gregson's view of the matter," Holmes observed. "Would you mind letting us know what you have seen and done?"

"I have no objection," Lestrade answered, seating himself. "I freely confess that I was of the opinion that Stangerson was concerned in the death of Drebber. This fresh development has shown me that I was completely mistaken. Full of the one idea, I set myself to find out what had become of the secretary. They had been seen together at Euston Station about half past eight on the evening of the third. At two in the morning Drebber had been found in the Brixton Road. The question which confronted me was to find out how Stangerson had been employed between 8.30 and the time of the crime, and what had become of him afterwards. I telegraphed to Liverpool, giving a description of the man, and warning them to keep a watch upon the American boats. I then set to work calling upon all the hotels and lodging houses in the vicinity of Euston. You see, I argued that if Drebber and his companion had become separated, the natural course for the latter would be to put up somewhere in the area for the night, and then to hang about the station again next morning."

"They would be likely to agree on some meeting place beforehand," remarked Holmes.

"So it proved. I spent the whole of yesterday evening in making enquiries entirely without avail. This morning I began very early, and at eight o'clock I reached Halliday's Private Hotel, in Little George Street. On my enquiry as to whether a Mr. Stangerson was living there, they at once answered me that he was.

"'No doubt you are the gentleman whom he was expecting,' they said. 'He has been waiting for a gentleman for two days.'

"'Where is he now?' I asked.

"'He is upstairs in bed. He wished to be called at nine.'

"'I will go up and see him at once,' I said.

"It seemed to me that my sudden appearance might shake his nerves and lead him to say something unguarded. His room was on the second floor, and there was a small corridor leading up to it. I was approaching the room when I saw something that made me feel sickish, in spite of my twenty years' experience. From under the door there curled a little red ribbon of blood, which had flowed across the hall and formed a little pool on the other side. The door was locked on the inside, but I put my shoulders to it, and knocked it in. The window of the room was open, and beside the window, all huddled up, lay the body of a man in his nightdress. He was quite dead, and had been for some time, for his limbs were rigid and cold. The man from the hotel later recognized him at once as being the same gentleman who had engaged the room under the name of Joseph Stangerson. The cause of death was a deep stab in the left side, which must have penetrated the heart. And now comes the strangest part of the affair. What do you suppose was above the murdered man?"

I felt a creeping of the flesh even before Sherlock Holmes answered.

"The word RACHE, written in letters of blood," he said.

"That was it," said Lestrade, in an awestruck voice; and we were all silent for a while.

There was something so methodical and so incomprehensible about the deeds of this unknown assassin, that it imparted a fresh ghastliness to his crimes. My nerves, which were steady enough on the field of battle tingled as I thought of it.

"The man was seen," continued Lestrade. "A

milk boy, passing on his way to the dairy, happened to walk down the lane which leads from the back of the hotel. He noticed that a ladder, which usually lay there, was raised against one of the windows of the second floor, which was wide open. After passing, he looked back and saw a man descend the ladder. He came down so quietly and openly that the boy imagined him to be some carpenter at work in the hotel. He took no particular notice of him, beyond thinking in his own mind that it was early for him to be at work. He has an impression that the man was tall, had a reddish face, and was dressed in a long, brownish coat. He must have stayed in the room some little time after the murder, for we found blood stained water in the basin, where he had washed his hands, and marks on the sheets where he had deliberately wiped his knife."

I glanced at Holmes on hearing the description of the murderer, which tallied so exactly with his own. There was, however, no trace of exultation or satisfaction upon his face.

"Did you find nothing in the room which could furnish a clue to the murderer?" he asked.

"Nothing. Stangerson had Drebber's purse in his pocket, but it seems that this was usual, as he did all the paying. There was eighty odd pounds in it, but nothing had been taken. Whatever the motives of these extraordinary crimes, robbery is certainly not one of them. There were no papers in the murdered man's pocket, except a single telegram, dated from Cleveland about a month ago, and containing the words, 'J. H. is in Europe.' There was no name appended to this message."

"And there was nothing else?" Holmes asked.

"Nothing of any importance. The man's novel, with which he had read himself to sleep, was lying upon the bed, and his pipe was on a chair beside him. There was a glass of water on the table, and on the window sill a small box containing a couple of pills."

Sherlock Holmes sprang from his chair with an exclamation of delight.

"The last link," he cried. "My case is complete."

The two detectives stared at him in amazement.

"I have now in my hands," my companion said, confidently, "all the threads which have formed such a tangle. There are, of course, details to be filled in, but I am as certain of all the main facts, from the time that Drebber parted from Stangerson at the station, up to the discovery of the body of the latter, as if I had seen them with my own eyes. I will give you a proof of my knowledge. Could you lay your hand upon those pills?"

"I have them," said Lestrade, producing a small white box; "I took them and the purse and the telegram, intending to have them put in a place of safety at the Police Station. It was the merest chance my taking these pills, for I am bound to say that I do not attach any importance to them."

"Give them here," said Holmes. "Now, Doctor," turning to me, "are those ordinary pills?"

They certainly were not. They were of a pearly grey color, small, round, and almost transparent against the light. "From their lightness and transparency, I should imagine that they are soluble in water," I remarked.

"Precisely so," answered Holmes. "Now would you mind going down and fetching that poor little devil of a terrier which has been bad so long, and which the landlady wanted you to deal with yesterday."

I went downstairs and carried the dog upstairs in my arms. It had been injured quite badly, likely hit by a passing cab, and did not have long to live. Yet it was in so much discomfort that our landlady asked us me to have mercy on it and take it out of its pain. I admit I had been putting it off, reluctant to perform the task, even though I knew it was the kindest thing. I placed it upon a cushion on the rug.

"I will now cut one of these pills in two," said Holmes, and immediately did so with his penknife. "One half we return into the box for future purposes. The other half I will place in this wine glass, in which is a teaspoonful of water. You perceive that our friend, the Doctor, is right, and that it readily dissolves."

"This may be very interesting," said Lestrade, in the injured tone of one who suspects that he is being laughed at, "I cannot see, however, what it has to do with the death of Mr. Joseph Stangerson."

"Patience, my friend, patience! You will find in time that it has everything to do with it. I shall now add a little milk to make the mixture palatable, and on presenting it to the dog we find that he laps it up readily enough."

As he spoke he spilled the contents of the wine glass into a saucer and placed it in front of the terrier, who speedily licked it dry. Sherlock Holmes' earnest demeanor had so far convinced us that we all sat in silence, watching the animal intently, and expecting some startling effect. Nothing happened, however. The dog continued to lie stretched upon the cushion, breathing in a labored way, but apparently neither the better nor the worse for its drink.

Holmes had taken out his watch, and as minute followed minute without result, an expression of the utmost disappointment appeared upon his features. He bit his lip, drummed his fingers upon the table, and showed every other symptom of acute impatience. So great was his emotion, that I felt sincerely sorry for him, while the two detectives smiled derisively, clearly pleased by his failure.

"It can't be a coincidence," he cried, at last springing from his chair and pacing wildly up and down the room; "it is impossible that it should be a mere coincidence. The very pills which I suspected in the case of Drebber are actually found after the death of Stangerson. And yet they are inert. What can it mean? Surely my whole chain of reasoning cannot have been false. It is impossible! And yet this wretched dog is none the worse. Ah, I have it! I have it!" With a perfect shriek of delight he rushed to the box, cut the other pill in two, dissolved it, added milk, and presented it to the terrier. The unfortunate creature's tongue seemed hardly to have been moistened before it gave a convulsive shiver in every limb, and lay as rigid and lifeless as if it had been struck by lightning.

Sherlock Holmes drew a long breath, and wiped the perspiration from his forehead. "I should have more faith," he said. "I ought to know by this time that when a fact appears to be opposed to a long train of deductions, it always proves to have some other explanation. Of the two pills in that box one was of the most deadly poison, and the other was entirely harmless. I ought to have known that before ever I saw the box at all."

This last statement appeared to me to be so startling, that I could hardly believe that he was in his sober senses. There was the dead dog, however, to prove that his guess had been correct. It seemed to me that the mists in my own mind were gradually clearing away, and I began to have a dim view of the truth.

"All this seems strange to you," continued Holmes, "because you failed at the beginning of the inquiry to grasp the importance of the single real clue which was presented to you. I had the good fortune to seize upon that, and everything which has occurred since then has served to confirm my original conclusion. Hence things which have confused you and made the case more obscure, only served to enlighten me and to strengthen my conclusions. It is a mistake to confuse strangeness with mystery. The most commonplace crime is often the most mysterious because it presents no new or special features from which deductions may be drawn. This murder would have been infinitely more difficult to unravel had the body of the victim been simply found lying in the roadway without any of those sensational details which have made it remarkable. These strange details, far from making the case more difficult, have really had the effect of making it less so."

Mr. Gregson, who had listened to this address with considerable impatience, could contain himself no longer. "Look here, Mr. Sherlock Holmes," he said, "we are all ready to acknowledge that you are a smart man, and that you have your own methods of working. We want something more than mere theory and preaching now, though. It is a case of taking the man. I have made my case out, and it seems I was wrong. Young Charpentier could not have been engaged in this second affair. Lestrade went after his man, Stangerson, and it appears that he was wrong too. You have thrown out hints here, and hints there, and seem to know more than we do, but the time has come when we feel that we have a right to ask you straight how much you do know of the business. Can you name the man who did it?"

"I cannot help feeling that Gregson is right, sir," remarked Lestrade. "We have both tried, and we have both failed. You have remarked more than once since I have been in the room that you had all the evidence which you require. Surely you will not withhold it any longer."

"Any delay in arresting the assassin," I observed, "might give him time to perpetrate some fresh atrocity."

Thus pressed by us all, Holmes showed signs of irresolution. He continued to walk up and down the room with his head sunk on his chest and his brows drawn down, as was his habit when lost in thought.

"There will be no more murders," he said at last, stopping abruptly and facing us. "That is out of the question. You have asked me if I know the name of the assassin. I do. The mere knowing of his name is a small thing, however, compared with the power of laying our hands upon him. This I expect very shortly to do. I have good hopes of managing it through my own arrangements; but it is a thing which needs delicate handling, for we have a shrewd and desperate man to deal with. And he is supported by another who is as clever as himself. As long as this man has no idea that anyone has a clue about him then there is some chance of securing him. But if he had the slightest suspicion, he would change his name, and vanish in an instant among the four million inhabitants of this great city.

"Without meaning to hurt either of your feelings, I am bound to say that I consider these men to be more than a match for the official force, and that is why I have not asked your assistance. If I fail I shall, of course, incur all the blame due to this omission; but I am prepared for that. At present I am ready to promise that the instant that I can communicate with you without endangering my own plans, I shall do so."

Gregson and Lestrade seemed to be far from satisfied by this assurance, or by his attitude toward the police. Gregson had flushed up to the roots of his flaxen hair, while Lestrade's beady eyes glistened with curiosity and resentment. Neither of them had time to speak, however, before there was a tap at the door, and the spokesman of the street kids, young Wiggins, introduced his small, dirty person.

"Please, sir," he said, "I have the cab downstairs."

"Good boy," said Holmes, blandly. "Why don't you introduce this pattern at Scotland Yard?" he said to the two detectives, taking a pair of steel handcuffs from a drawer. "See how beautifully the spring works. They fasten in an instant."

"The old pattern is good enough," remarked Lestrade, "if we can only find the man to put them on."

"Very good, very good," said Holmes, smiling. "The cabman may as well help me with my boxes. Just ask him to step up, Wiggins."

I was surprised to find my companion speaking as though he were about to set out on a journey, since he had not said anything to me about it. There was a small trunk in the room, and this he pulled out and began to strap together. He was busily engaged at it when the cabman entered the room.

"Just give me a help with this buckle, cabman," he said, kneeling over his task, and never turning his head.

The fellow came forward with a somewhat sullen, defiant air, and put down his hands to assist. At that instant there was a sharp click, the jangling of metal, and Sherlock Holmes sprang to his feet again.

"Gentlemen," he cried, with flashing eyes, "let me introduce you to Mr. Jefferson Hope, the murderer of Enoch Drebber and of Joseph Stangerson."

The whole thing occurred in a moment—so quickly that I had no time to realize it. I have a vivid recollection of that instant, of Holmes' triumphant expression and the ring of his voice, of the cabman's dazed, savage face, as he glared at the glittering handcuffs, which had appeared as if by magic upon his wrists. For a second or two we might have been a group of statues. Then, with a roar of fury, the prisoner wrenched himself free from Holmes's grasp, and hurled himself through the window. Woodwork and glass broke before him; but before he got quite through, Gregson, Lestrade, and Holmes sprang upon him like so many hounds. He was dragged back into the room, and then commenced a terrific fight. So powerful and so fierce was he that the four of us were shaken off again and again. It was not until Lestrade succeeded in getting his hand around his neck and half strangling him that we made him realize that his struggles were of no avail. Even then we felt no security until we had fastened his feet as well as his hands. That done, we rose to our feet breathless and panting.

"We have his cab," said Sherlock Holmes. "It will serve to take him to Scotland Yard. And now, gentlemen," he continued, with a pleasant smile, "we have reached the end of our little mystery. You are very welcome to put any questions that you like to me now, and there is no danger that I will refuse to answer them."

Our prisoner's furious resistance did not apparently indicate any anger towards ourselves, for on finding himself powerless, he smiled in an affable manner, and expressed his hopes that he had not hurt any of us in the scuffle. "I guess you're going to take me to the police station," he remarked to Sherlock Holmes. "My cab's at the door. If you'll loosen my legs I'll walk down to it. I'm not so light to lift as I used to be."

Gregson and Lestrade exchanged glances as if they thought this proposition rather a bold one. But Holmes at once took the prisoner at his word, and loosened the towel which we had tied around his ankles. He rose and stretched his legs, as though to assure himself that they were free once more. I remember that I thought to myself, as I eyed him, that I had seldom seen a more powerfully built man; and his dark sunburned face bore an expression of determination and energy which was as formidable as his personal strength.

"If there's a vacant place for a chief of the

police, I reckon you are the man for it," he said, gazing with admiration at Holmes. "The way you kept on my trail was impressive."

"You had better come with me," said Holmes to the two detectives.

"I can drive you," said Lestrade.

"Good! and Gregson can come inside with me. You too, Doctor, you have taken an interest in the case and may as well stick to us."

I gladly agreed, and we all descended together. Our prisoner made no attempt at escape, but stepped calmly into the cab which had been his, and we followed him. Lestrade mounted the box, whipped up the horse, and brought us in a very short time to the Yard. We were ushered into a small chamber where a police inspector noted down our prisoner's name and the names of the men with whose murder he had been charged. The inspector was a white faced, unemotional man, who went through his duties in a dull mechanical way. "The prisoner will be put before the judge in the course of the week," he said. "In the mean time, Mr. Jefferson Hope, have you anything that you wish to say? I must warn you that your words will be taken down, and may be used against you."

"I've got a good deal to say," our prisoner said slowly. "I want to tell you gentlemen all about it."

"Hadn't you better reserve that for your trial?" asked the Inspector.

"I may never be tried," he answered. "You needn't look startled. It isn't suicide I am thinking of. Are you a doctor?" He turned his fierce dark eyes upon me as he asked this last question.

"Yes; I am," I answered.

"Then put your hand here," he said, with a smile, motioning towards his chest.

I did so; and became at once aware of an extraordinary throbbing and commotion which was going on inside. The walls of his chest seemed to quiver as a frail building would do inside when some powerful engine was at work. In the silence of the room I could hear a dull humming and buzzing noise coming from his heart.

"Why," I cried, "you have an aortic aneurism!"

"That's what they call it," he said, placidly. "I went to a Doctor last week about it, and he told me that it is bound to burst before many days passed. It has been getting worse for years. I got it from over exposure and under feeding among the Salt Lake Mountains. I've done my work now, and I don't care how soon I go, but I should like to leave some account of the business behind me. I don't want to be remembered as a common cut-throat."

The inspector and the two detectives had a hurried discussion as to the advisability of allowing him to tell his story.

"Do you consider, Doctor, that there is immediate danger?" the inspector asked.

"Most certainly there is," I answered.

"In that case it is clearly our duty, in the interests of justice, to take his statement," said the inspector. "You are at liberty, sir, to give your account, which I again warn you will be taken down."

"I'll sit down, with your leave," the prisoner said, taking a seat. "This aneurism of mine makes me easily tired, and the tussle we had half an hour ago has not helped. I'm on the brink of the grave, and I am not likely to lie to you. Every word I say is the absolute truth, and how you use it is a matter of no consequence to me.

"It don't much matter to you why I hated these men," he said; "it's enough that they were guilty of the death of two human beings—a father and a daughter—and that they had, therefore, forfeited their own lives. After the lapse of time that has passed since their crime, it was impossible for me to secure a conviction against them in any court. I knew of their guilt though, and I determined that I should be judge, jury, and executioner all rolled into one. You'd have done the same, if you have any manhood in you, if you had been in my place."

Sherlock's eyes sparkled as he looked toward the prisoner. "Come, Mr. Hope. By your own admission you may not live to see trial. This is your own chance to tell your story. I beg you to tell it all and not leave a single important detail untold.

Jefferson Hope poured himself a glass of water and leaned back in his chair. "Very well," he said, "I will start at the beginning. Have any of you ever heard of a man named John Ferrier?"

We all shook our heads.

"How about the Avenging Angels?"

Again we all shook our heads no. All of us, that is, except for Holmes, who nodded slowly and gestured for Mr. Hope to continue.

CHAPTER VIII.
THE PRISONERS TALE

THE first part of the story I heard from the very lips of John Ferrier and I'll tell it over to you as best I can. It was in the year 1847 and John Ferrier, along with twenty others, formed a wagon train heading west to California. The group was ill prepared and found themselves in one of the driest parts of the country without enough water. Of the twenty-one that started, pretty soon there were only two left, John Ferrier and a young girl named Lucy. John's wife and Lucy's parents all died in the journey. And it looked to John that he and Lucy didn't have long to live either, having no water and no means of getting any.

The buzzards had already begun circling the two when a great cloud of dust rose up in the east. Ten thousand men, women, and children were riding toward them, taking with them all they had. A couple of them saw John and Lucy lying beside the road and stopped to give them water. They asked who he was and he told them.

"And is she your daughter?" They asked, pointing to the girl.

"I guess she is now," Ferrier said. "She's mine

cause I saved her and no man will take her from me. She's Lucy Ferrier from this day on. Who are you, though?"

"We are the disciples of Joseph Smith."

"You are the Mormons?" Ferrier said.

"We are the Mormons."

"And where are you going."

"We do not know. We are led by our Prophet, Brigham Young. You must come before him. He shall say what is to be done with you."

They brought him to the largest wagon, and presented the matter before their prophet. "If we take you with us," he said, in solemn words, "it can only be as believers in our own creed. We shall have no wolves in our fold. It would be better that your bones should bleach in this wilderness than that you should prove to be that little speck of decay which in time corrupts the whole fruit. Will you come with us on these terms?"

"Guess I'll come with you on any terms," said Ferrier, with such emphasis that the grave Elders could not restrain a smile. The leader alone retained his stern, impressive expression.

"Take him, Brother Stangerson," he said, "give him food and drink, and the child too. Let it be your task also to teach him our holy creed. We have delayed long enough. Forward! On, on to Zion!"

Well, it only took John and Lucy a couple of days to recover. The Mormons soon became quite glad they had come across them, for once John Ferrier was feeling well again, he proved to be as able a man as any of them. He knew the terrain, was an excellent guide, and an exceptional hunter. When the group reached Utah, Brigham Young announced they had arrived at their destination, and he set about making maps and dividing up the land. Ferrier had made such an impression by this point that he was given a piece of land as large and fertile as any of the settlers, save of course for Brigham Young himself and the four principal Elders, who were Stangerson, Kemball, Johnston, and Drebber.

John Ferrier was a man of a practical turn of mind, keen in his dealings and skillful with his hands. His iron constitution let him work morning and evening at improving and tilling his lands. Hence it came about that his farm and all that belonged to him prospered exceedingly. In three years he was better off than his neighbors, in six he was well-to-do, in nine he was rich, and in twelve there were not half a dozen men in the whole of Salt Lake City who could compare with him.

There was only one way he offended the Mormons, and that was by never taking a wife. The Mormons were determined to grow in size and instituted what they called plural marriage in order to raise up the seed of their people, with no limits upon the number of wives a man could take. It's what John Ferrier called polygamy and he wanted nothing to do with marriage amongst the Mormons, either for himself or for his daughter Lucy. He never mentioned this to any of the Mormons however. They never took issue with it, save to look at John as a little queer because he didn't want to take a wife. It only became an issue once Lucy grew up and reached a marriageable age herself.

This is where I come into the story. I was out in the Nevada mountains prospecting for silver and had ridden into Salt Lake City with a few friends trying to raise the capital to work a couple of silver loads we discovered. Lucy had grown into quite a young woman at this point. I first saw her when she was riding from her farm into town on her own, and came to a place where her path was blocked by a herd of cattle. There was a little gap, and she tried to ride through, but no sooner had she moved forward than the gap closed and she found herself surrounded by longhorns. She would have been alright, for she was a skilled rider, but her horse got scared and started jumping about. It was a tight situation, each time the horse jumped it hit the horns of one of the cattle, and each time it hit the horns it jumped. Had she been shaken off the horse, it would have been the end of her. Now I happened to be about and rode through to her, and gradually led her horse away from danger.

"You're not hurt, I hope, miss," said I.

She looked up at me and laughed lightly. "I'm awful frightened," she said. "Whoever would have thought that Poncho would have been so scared by a lot of cows?"

"It's good you kept your seat," said I. "I guess you are the daughter of John Ferrier. I saw you ride down from his house. When you see him, ask him if he remembers the Hopes of St. Louis. If he's the same Ferrier, my father and he were pretty thick."

"Hadn't you better come and ask yourself?" she asked.

Well I admit I was awfully glad at the suggestion for I was mighty happy to get to know her a bit better. "I'll do so," I said, "but I've been in the mountains for two months, and am not over and above in visiting condition. He must take me as he finds me."

"He has a good deal to thank you for, and so have I," she answered. "He's awful fond of me. If those cows had jumped on me he'd have never got over it."

"Neither would I," I said.

"You! Well, I don't see that it would make much matter to you, anyhow. You ain't even a friend of ours." Now I must have shown how much her words hurt because she laughed. "There, I didn't mean that," she said; "of course, you are a friend now. You must come and see us. Now I must push along, or father won't trust me with his business any more. Good-bye!"

Well, I need hardly tell you gentlemen that call upon the Ferriers I did, that very night and many times afterwards as well. It didn't take me long to fall completely in love with Lucy and her with me. At first I feared that my advances would be rejected, me not being a Mormon. But as I was soon to learn, and as I've already told you gentlemen, John Ferrier had no intention of marrying his daughter to a Mormon and was quite keen to have me as a son in law.

But of course a man can't just take a wife without the means to provide for her. My friends and I had raised the money we needed to work our silver loads, and it was time to head back to Nevada. "I am off, Lucy," I told her, taking her two hands in mine. "I won't ask you to come with me now, but will you be ready to come with me when I return?"

"And when will that be?" she asked.

"A couple of months at the outside. I will come and claim you then, my darling. There's no one who can stand between us."

"And how about father?" she asked.

"He has given his consent, provided we get these mines working all right. I have no fear on that account."

"Oh, well, if you and father have arranged it all, there's no more to be said."

"It is settled, then. The longer I stay, the harder it will be to go. They are waiting for me at the canyon. Good-bye, my own darling—good-bye. In two months you shall see me."

Now things clearly did not turn out the way I hoped or else I should not be a prisoner today. As I said, the locals were willing to forgive John Ferrier for not marrying himself. I think they imagined his heart had once been broken and could never bring himself to marry again. However, they were not so forgiving when it came to his daughter. Not only was she beautiful, but she was the sole heir to all of Ferrier's fortune, and considered to be quite a desirable match. I don't know how they learned about our engagement, but I had only been gone three weeks when John Ferrier came home one day to find the Elder Stangerson, the very man who had looked after him on their journey west, waiting for him.

"Brother Ferrier," he said, "the true believers have been good friends to you. We picked you up when you were starving in the desert, we shared our food with you, led you safe to the Chosen Valley, gave you a goodly share of land where you became rich under our protection. Is not this so?"

"It is so," answered John Ferrier.

"In return for all this we asked but one condition: that was, that you should embrace the true faith, and conform in every way to its usages. This you promised to do, and this, if common report says truly, you have neglected."

"And how have I neglected it?" asked Ferrier. "Have I not given to the common fund? Have I not attended at the Temple? Have I not—?"

"Where are your wives?" asked Stangerson, looking round him. "Call them in, that I may greet them."

"It is true that I have not married," Ferrier answered. "But women were few, and there were many who had better claims than I. I was not a lonely man; I had my daughter to attend to my wants."

"It is of that daughter that I would speak to you. She has grown to be the flower of Utah, and has found favor in the eyes of many who are high in the land. There are stories of her which I would rather disbelieve—stories that she is engaged to some nonbeliever. This must be the gossip of idle tongues. For it is impossible that you, who profess the holy creed, should suffer your daughter to violate it."

Ferrier said nothing. Though he appreciated the help Stangerson had given him in the desert, he did not approve of the man, who was brutish and had a violent temper. He would have turned him out of the house, but knew Stangerson was one of the four elders of the Danites—a man who had power and was not afraid to use it.

"Upon this one point your whole faith shall be tested," Stangerson continued. "Thus it has been decided in the Sacred Council of Four. The girl is young, and we would not have her wed grey hairs, neither would we deprive her of all choice. I myself have a son, and Drebber has a son as well, and either of them would gladly welcome your daughter to their house. Let her choose between them. They are young and rich, and of the true faith. What say you to that?"

"You will give us time," Ferrier said at last. "My daughter is very young—she is scarcely of an age to marry."

"She shall have a month to choose," said Stangerson. "At the end of that time she shall give her answer."

All of this I learned later from Lucy, who as it turned out was in the house at the time and overheard the whole conversation. She ran up to her father after Stangerson left and said, "I could not help hearing. His voice rang through the house. Oh, father, father, what shall we do?"

"Don't you scare yourself," he answered. "We'll fix it up somehow or another. You don't find your fancy kind o' lessening for this chap, do you? No, of course not. I shouldn't care to hear you say you did. There's a party starting for Nevada tomorrow, and I'll manage to send him a message letting him know the hole we are in. If I know anything o' that young man, he'll be back here with a speed that would whip electro-telegraphs. When he comes, he will advise us for the best. But it is for you that I am frightened, dear. We made a promise to keep by their ways, and there may be more than a bit of trouble if we break it. But we haven't broken it yet. We have a clear month before us; at the end of that, I guess we had best slip out of Utah."

"Leave Utah!"

"That's about the size of it."

"But the farm?"

"We will raise as much as we can in money, and

let the rest go. To tell the truth, Lucy, it isn't the first time I have thought of doing it. I'm a freeborn American, and all their ways are new to me. Guess I'm too old to learn."

"But they won't let us leave," she said.

"Wait till Jefferson comes, and we'll soon manage that. In the meantime, don't you fret yourself, my dearie, and don't get your eyes swelled up. There's nothing to be afeared about, and there's no danger at all."

CHAPTER IX.
A FLIGHT FOR LIFE

THE very next day John Ferrier went into town and when he came back there were two horses tied up at his gate. Entering his house, he saw two young men sitting at his table like they owned the place; these very two men I have finally tracked down and killed here in London.

"We have come," the younger Stangerson said, "at the advice of our fathers to ask the hand of your daughter. You and she may choose whichever one of us seems better for her. Though as I have but one wife and Brother Drebber here already has two, it appears to me that my claim is the stronger one."

"Nay, nay, Brother Stangerson," cried Drebber; "the question is not how many wives we have, but how many we can keep. My father has now given over his mills to me, and I am the richer man."

"But my prospects are better," said the other, warmly. "When my father dies I shall have his tanning yard and his leather factory. Then I am your elder, and am higher in the Church."

"It will be for the girl to decide," said Drebber. "We will leave it all to her decision."

"Look here," John Ferrier said. "When my daughter summons you, you can come, but until then I don't want to see your faces again."

The two young Mormons stared at him in amazement. In their eyes this competition between them for the girl's hand was the highest of honors both to her and her father.

"There are two ways out of the room," cried Ferrier; "there is the door, and there is the window. Which do you care to use?" The two ran out the door and he called after them, "Let me know when you have settled which it is to be."

Stangerson cried out, white with rage. "You shall rue this to the end of your days."

"The young canting rascals!" he said to Lucy after they had gone. "I would sooner see you in your grave, my girl, than the wife of either of them."

"And so should I, father," she answered, "but Jefferson will soon be here."

"Yes. It will not be long before he comes. The sooner the better, for we do not know what their next move may be."

But as it turned out, the message was late in getting to me. Now's as good a time as any to tell you gentlemen what it is that had these two so scared. There's a group officially known as the Danite Band, but more commonly referred to as the Avenging Angels. There were many rumors about this Mormon group of vigilantes and I used to think there wasn't much truth in the stories, that they were just made up to scare people into line. But the morning after John Ferrier chased Stangerson and Drebber from his house, he got his first proof that there was plenty of truth to the rumors. He awoke to find a note attached to his sheets that said:

"Twenty-nine days are given you for amendment, and then—"

I think the dash probably gave him a greater scare than any threat would have. He was mighty upset about how this note could have gotten into his bedroom, for he had made sure to lock all the windows and doors the night before. He threw away the paper and said nothing to Lucy, but he couldn't drive it from his mind. He remembered that he'd been given 30 days to choose an acceptable husband for Lucy and as the note made perfectly clear, he only had 29 left.

The next morning was even worse when he woke to find the number 28 on the ceiling, drawn with what looked like a burnt stick. He next morning it was followed by a 27 painted above the door. So it was each day that followed, and each day they hoped for my arrival. But as I said, the note was delayed in reaching me.

I rode like the wind, not stopping to eat or sleep. I arrived on the very last night and saw that these Avenging Angels had set up a perimeter around the farm. I crawled on my belly across the yard and knocked quietly upon the window of Ferrier's room. He let me in the window and cried out "How you scared me! Whatever made you come in like that."

"Give me food," I said. "I have had no time for bite or sup for eight-and-forty hours." Once I filled my belly, I asked "Does Lucy bear up well?"

"Yes. She does not know the danger."

"That is well. The house is watched on every side. That is why I crawled my way up to it. They may be darned sharp, but they're not quite sharp enough to catch a Washoe hunter."

"You're a man to be proud of," he said to me. "There are not many who would come to share our danger and our troubles."

"You've hit it there, partner. I have a respect for you, but if you were alone in this business I'd think twice before I put my head into such a hornet's nest. It's Lucy that brings me here, and before harm comes on her I guess there will be one less of the Hope family in Utah."

"What are we to do?"

"Tomorrow is your last day, and unless you act tonight you are lost. I have a mule and two horses waiting in the Eagle Canyon. How much money have you?"

"Two thousand dollars in gold, and five in notes."

"That will do. I have as much more to add to it. We must push for Carson City through the mountains. You had best wake Lucy."

While Ferrier was getting Lucy ready, I packed all the food I could into a small parcel, and filled a stoneware jar with water, for I knew by experience that the mountain wells were few and far between.

"We must make our start at once," I said as soon as Ferrier came back with Lucy. "The front and back entrances are watched, but with caution we may get away through the side window and across the fields. Once on the road we are only two miles from the Canyon where the horses are waiting. By daybreak we should be half-way through the mountains."

"What if we are stopped?" asked Ferrier.

I slapped the butt of my revolver. "If they are too many for us, we shall take two or three of them with us."

I opened the window and waited until a dark cloud blocked the moon, then slowly crawled out. One by one we passed through the little garden until we came to the shelter of a hedge. We had just got covered when I heard someone coming and pulled Ferrier and Lucy into the shadows. There was a hoot of a mountain owl a few yards away from us, answered by another hoot at a small distance. Then two men came together, standing in the very gap we were intending to run through.

"Tomorrow at midnight," said the man who appeared to be in charge. "When the Whip-poor-Will calls three times."

"It is well," returned the other. "Shall I tell Brother Drebber?"

"Pass it on to him, and from him to the others. Nine to seven!"

"Seven to five!" repeated the other, and the two figures flitted away in different directions. Their words were obviously some form of sign and countersign. The instant that their footsteps had died away in the distance, I jumped to my feet and all three of us were through the gap.

"Hurry on! hurry on!" I called from time to time. "We are through the line of sentinels. Everything depends on speed. Hurry on!"

Once on the high road we made rapid progress. Only once did we meet anyone, and then we managed to slip into a field, and so avoid recognition. Before reaching the town I broke off onto a rugged and narrow footpath which led to the mountains. This brought us to Eagle Canyon, where the horses were waiting.

The path was so narrow in places that we had to travel one at a time, and it was so rough that if all three of us hadn't been strong riders we couldn't have traversed it at all. Yet in spite of all dangers and difficulties, our hearts were light within us, for every step increased the distance between us and what we were running from.

But just as we thought we were away, we had a proof that we were still within their territory. We had reached the very wildest and most desolate portion of the pass when the girl gave a startled cry, and pointed upwards. On a rock overlooking the track there stood a solitary sentinel. He saw us as soon as we saw him, and his call of "Who goes there?" rang through the silent ravine.

"Travelers for Nevada," said I, with my hand upon the rifle, just in case.

"By whose permission?" he asked.

"The Holy Four," answered Ferrier. His Mormon experiences had taught him that that was the highest authority to which he could refer.

"Nine from seven," cried the sentinel.

"Seven from five," I returned, remembering the countersign which I had heard in the garden.

"Pass, and the Lord go with you," said the voice from above. Beyond his post the path broadened out, and the horses were able to break into a trot. Looking back, we could see the solitary watcher leaning upon his gun, and knew that we had passed their final outpost, and that freedom lay before us.

CHAPTER X.
THE AVENGING ANGELS

WE rode all night, and when morning broke, we saw that we were hemmed in by snow capped peaks all around us. We stopped only long enough for a quick breakfast and then were off again. "They will be upon our track by this time," I said. "Everything depends upon our speed. Once safe in Carson we may rest for the remainder of our lives."

During the whole of that day we struggled on, and by evening we must have been thirty miles from our enemies. At night we found a spot at the base of a cliff where rocks offered some protection from the chill wind, and there we huddled together for warmth to enjoy a few hours' sleep. Before daybreak, however, we were up and on our way once more. We had seen no signs of any pursuers, and I began to think that they were fairly out of their reach. Little did I know how far they could reach or how soon they were to close upon us.

The middle of the second day we began to run out of food. This didn't worry me, however, for there was game to be had among the mountains, and I had frequently before had to depend upon my rifle for the needs of life. We were now nearly five thousand feet above the sea level, and the air was bitter. I found a sheltered spot, make a quick fire, and left Ferrier and Lucy there to keep warm. Then I threw my gun over my shoulder, and set out in search of whatever chance might throw in my way.

I walked for a couple of miles through one ravine after another without success. At last, after two or three hours' fruitless search, I saw a big horn sheep and hit it with my first shot. The creature was too unwieldy to lift, so I contented myself with cutting away one haunch and part of the flank. I then tried to retrace my steps, for the evening was already drawing in. But I had gone too far, leaving the ravines I knew well, and it was no easy thing to find my way back. I went on for a mile or so before coming to a stream that I was sure I'd never seen before. I went back and tried another trail, but with the same result. It was almost dark before I found a ravine that was familiar. I was tired and carrying a heavy load, but kept going, knowing that every step brought me closer to Lucy.

By the time I got back I had been gone nearly five hours. I gave a call, but heard only an echo for a reply. I shouted louder, but again nothing. A dread came over me and I dropped the food and began to run. I soon came full in sight of the spot where the fire had been lit. There was still a glowing pile of wood ashes there, but it had evidently not been tended since I left. The same dead silence still reigned all round. There was no living creature near the remains of the fire: animals, Ferrier, and Lucy were all gone.

I grabbed a half burnt piece of wood from the smoldering fire, blew it into a flame, and examined the camp. The ground was all stamped down by the feet of horses. The direction of their tracks proved that they had afterwards turned back to Salt Lake City. At first I thought they had carried Ferrier and Lucy back with them, but then my eye fell on a heap of freshly dug soil. A stick had been planted above the newly dug grave with a piece of paper attached that read:

> JOHN FERRIER,
> FORMERLY OF SALT LAKE CITY
> Died August 4th, 1860.

The sturdy old man, whom I had left so short a time before, was gone, then, and this was all that remained. I looked around to see if there was a second grave, but there was no sign of one. Lucy had been carried back by our pursuers to becoming part of one of their harems. At the time, I wished I was lying myself besides the old farmer in my last silent resting place. But I shook that off quickly enough and set my mind on revenge. I went back and found the food I had dropped, stirred up the remains of the fire, and cooked myself enough to last several days. I then set back through the mountains on the trail of the avenging angels.

For five days I walked, footsore and weary, through the trails I had already taken on horseback. At night I flung myself down among the rocks, and snatched a few hours of sleep; but before daybreak I was always well on my way. On the sixth day, I reached Eagle Canyon, and from there looked down upon the home of the Mormons. Worn and exhausted, I leaned upon my rifle and saw flags and banners in some of the streets and other signs of a festival. I was still wondering what this might mean when I heard the clatter of horse's hoofs, and saw a mounted man riding towards me. As he approached, I recognized him as a Mormon named Cowper, to whom I had rendered services at different times. I therefore called out to him, with the object of finding out what Lucy Ferrier's fate had been.

"I am Jefferson Hope," he said. "You remember me."

The Mormon looked at me with astonishment. "You are mad to come here," he cried. "It is as much as my own life is worth to be seen talking with you. There is a warrant against you from the Holy Four for assisting the Ferriers away."

"I don't fear them, or their warrant," I said. "You must know something of this matter, Cowper. I ask you by everything you hold dear to answer a few questions. We have always been friends, don't refuse to answer me."

"What is it?" the Mormon asked uneasily. "Be quick. The very rocks have ears and the trees eyes."

"What has become of Lucy Ferrier?"

"She was married yesterday to young Drebber. Hold up, man, hold up, you have no life left in you!"

"Don't mind me. Married, you say?"

"Married yesterday—that's what those flags are for on the Endowment House. There were some words between young Drebber and young Stangerson as to which was to have her. They'd both been in the party that followed them, and Stangerson had shot her father, which seemed to give him the best claim; but when they argued it out in council, Drebber's party was the stronger, so he got her. He won't have her very long though, for I saw death in her face yesterday. She is more like a ghost than a woman. Are you off, then?"

"Yes, I am off."

"Where are you going?"

"Never mind," I answered; and, slinging my rifle over my shoulder, I strode off down the gorge and so away into the heart of the mountains. Amongst all the wild beasts out there, I doubt there were any so fierce and dangerous as myself. There I hid, gathering what news I could, waiting for my chance. But Cowper's words were only too right. Between the terrible death of her father and the hateful marriage into which she had been forced, poor Lucy never held up her head again. She pined away and died within a month. When I heard of her death, I had to come see her, even at the risk of my life.

I found where they had laid her body while it awaited burial. I kissed her on her cold forehead and saw a wedding ring on her finger—there was no way I would let her be buried in that. I took it with me and went back into the mountains. I waited for my chance. Once I shot at Stangerson through his window, but missed. Another time I hurled some rocks down a cliff at Drebber, but again missed. They were well protected during the day and too scared to go out at night, so it wasn't easy to get at them.

It became clear pretty soon that my health couldn't handle living out in the mountains too much longer and my money was running out. I got a job in the mines, expecting I'd be away for a year at most, but was gone nearly five. When I got back, I found out that there had been a falling out amongst the Mormons, and both Drebber and Stangerson were amongst those who left. Drebber left a wealthy man, but Stangerson had become poor and had gone into Drebber's employ.

It was many years before I got wind of them again. They had gone to Cleveland, Ohio, and there I found them, but I wasn't as careful as I should have been. I peaked in Drebber's window to be sure it was him, and he got a glimpse of me. Drebber had enough pull with the Cleveland police to have me arrested on some made up charge. The charge couldn't stick of course, but it was enough to get me held in custody for a few weeks. In that time they slipped away again, this time to Europe.

I didn't have enough money to chase after them, so had to find some work before I could continue my pursuit. When I finally got to St. Petersburg, they had left for Paris. In Paris I found they had gone to Copenhagen. From there I found that they had gone to London, and this time they weren't going to escape me.

CHAPTER XI.
THE MURDER

THEY were rich and I was poor, so that it was no easy matter for me to follow them. When I got to London my pocket was about empty. Driving and riding are as natural to me as walking, so I applied at a cab owner's office, and soon got employment. I was to bring a certain amount a week to the owner, and whatever was left over I might keep for myself. There was seldom much left over, but I managed to scrape along somehow. The hardest part was learning my way about, for of all the mazes that were ever designed, this city is the most confusing. I had a map beside me though, and when once I knew the principal hotels and stations, I got on pretty well.

It was some time before I found out where my two gentlemen were living; but I inquired and inquired until at last I dropped across them. They were at a boarding house at Camberwell, over on the other side of the river. When once I found them out I knew that I had them at my mercy. I had grown my beard, and there was no chance of their recognizing me. I would dog them and follow them until I saw my opportunity. I was determined that they should not escape me again.

Go where they would about London, I was always at their heels. Sometimes I followed them on my cab, and sometimes on foot, but the cab was the best, for then they could not get away from me. It was only early in the morning or late at night that I could earn anything, so that I began to get behind in payments to my employer. I did not mind that, however, as long as I could lay my hand upon the men I wanted.

They were very cunning, though. They must have thought that there was some chance of their being followed, for they would never go out alone, and never after nightfall. For two weeks I drove behind them every day, and never once saw them separate. Drebber was drunk half the time, but Stangerson was not to be caught napping. I watched them late and early, but never saw the ghost of a chance. But I was not discouraged, for something told me that the hour had almost come. My only fear was that this thing in my chest might burst a little too soon and leave my work undone.

At last, one evening I was driving up and down their street when I saw a cab drive up to their door. Some luggage was brought out, and after a time Drebber and Stangerson followed it, and drove off. I whipped up my horse and kept within sight of them, feeling very ill at ease, for I feared that they were going to move again. At Euston Station they got out, and I left a boy to hold my horse, and followed them on to the platform. I heard them ask for the Liverpool train, and the guard answer that one had just gone and there would not be another for some hours. Stangerson was upset at that, but Drebber seemed rather pleased. I got so close to them that I could hear every word that passed between them. Drebber said that he had a little business of his own to do, and he would soon rejoin him. Stangerson argued with him, and reminded him that they had resolved to stick together. Drebber answered that the matter was a delicate one, and that he must go alone. I could not catch what Stangerson said to that, but it seemed to anger Drebber, who burst out swearing. He reminded Stangerson that he was nothing more than his paid servant, and that he must not tell him what to do. Stangerson stopped arguing and told Drebber that if he should miss the last train, they would meet at Halliday's Private Hotel. Drebber answered that he would be back on the platform before eleven, and made his way out of the station.

The moment for which I had waited so long had at last come. I had my enemies within my power. Together they could protect each other, but singly they were at my mercy. My plans were already formed. There is no satisfaction in revenge unless the offender has time to realize who it is that strikes him, and why retribution has come upon him. I wanted the man who had wronged me to understand that his old sin had caught up to him. It chanced that some days before a gentleman whose job it was to tend to some houses in the Brixton Road had dropped the key to an empty house in my cab. I returned the key to him that same evening, but not until I'd had a copy made. Thus, I had at least one spot in this great city where I could be free from interruption. How to get Drebber to that house was the difficult problem that I now needed to solve.

He walked down the road and went into one or

two liquor shops, staying for nearly half-an-hour in the last of them. When he came out he staggered in his walk, and was evidently pretty drunk. There was a hansom just in front of me, and he hailed it. I followed it so close that the nose of my horse was within a yard of his driver the whole way. We rattled across Waterloo Bridge and through miles of streets, until, to my astonishment, we found ourselves back in his old rooms. I could not imagine what his intention was in returning there; but I went on and pulled up my cab a hundred yards or so from the house. He entered it, and his hansom drove away.

Well, I waited for a quarter of an hour, or more, when suddenly there came a noise like people fighting inside the house. Next moment the door was flung open and two men appeared, one of whom was Drebber, and the other was a young chap whom I had never seen before. This fellow had Drebber by the collar, and when they came to the head of the steps he gave him a shove and a kick which sent him half across the road. "You hound," he cried, shaking his stick at him; "I'll teach you to insult an honest girl!"' He was so hot that I think he would have thrashed Drebber with his cudgel, only that the cur ran away down the road as fast as his legs would carry him. He ran as far as the corner, and then, seeing my cab, he hailed me and jumped in. "Drive me to Halliday's Private Hotel," said he.

When I had him inside my cab, my heart jumped so with joy that I was afraid that at this last moment my aneurism might go wrong. I drove along slowly, weighing in my mind what was best to do. I might take him right out into the country, and there in some deserted lane have my last interview with him. I had almost decided upon this, when he solved the problem for me. The craze for drink had seized him again, and he ordered me to pull up outside a gin palace. He went in, leaving word that I should wait for him. There he remained until closing time, and when he came out he was so far gone that I knew the game was in my own hands.

Don't imagine that I intended to kill him in cold blood. It would only have been rigid justice if I had done so, but I could not bring myself to do it. I had long determined that he should have a chance for his life if he chose to take advantage of it. Among the many jobs I've filled in America during my wandering life, I was once janitor and sweeper in the laboratory at York College. One day the professor was lecturing on poisons, and he showed his students some alkaloid, as he called it, which he had extracted from some South American arrow poison, and which was so powerful that the least grain meant instant death. I spotted the bottle in which this was kept, and when they were all gone, I helped myself to a little of it. I made the poison into small pills and made similar pills without the poison. I determined that when I had my chance, the men should each have a chance to choose a pill out of one of these boxes, while I ate the pill that remained. From that day I always had my pill boxes about with me, and the time had now come when I was to use them.

It was nearer one than twelve, and a wild, bleak night, with strong wind and rain falling in torrents. Dismal as it was outside, I was glad within—so glad that I could have shouted out from pure joy. If any of you gentlemen have ever desired a thing, and longed for it during twenty long years, and then suddenly found it within your reach, you would understand my feelings. I lit a cigar, and puffed at it to steady my nerves, but my hands were trembling, and my temples throbbing with excitement. As I drove, I could see old John Ferrier and sweet Lucy looking at me out of the darkness and smiling at me, just as plain as I see you all in this room. All the way they were ahead of me, one on each side of the horse until I pulled up at the house in the Brixton Road.

There was not a soul to be seen, nor a sound to be heard, except the dripping of the rain. When I looked in at the window, I found Drebber all huddled together in a drunken sleep. I shook him by the arm, "It's time to get out," I said.

"All right, cabby," said he.

I suppose he thought we had come to the hotel that he had mentioned, for he got out without another word, and followed me down the garden. I had to walk beside him to keep him steady, for he was still a little top heavy. When we came to the door, I opened it, and led him into the front room. I give you my word that all the way, the father and the daughter were walking in front of us.

"It's infernally dark," said he, stamping about.

"We'll soon have a light," I said, striking a match and putting it to a wax candle which I had brought with me. "Now, Enoch Drebber," I continued, turning to him, and holding the light to my own face, "who am I?"

He gazed at me with drunken eyes for a moment, and then I saw a horror spring up in them, and convulse his whole features, which showed me that he knew me. He staggered back with a livid face, and I saw the sweat break out upon his brow, while his teeth chattered in his head. At the sight, I leaned my back against the door and laughed loud and long. I had always known that vengeance would be sweet, but I had never hoped it would be this sweet.

"You dog!" I said. "I have hunted you from Salt Lake City to St. Petersburg, and you have always escaped me. Now, at last your running from me has come to an end, because one of us will never see tomorrow's sun rise." He shrank still further away as I spoke, and I could see on his face that he thought I was mad. And at the time perhaps I was. The pulses in my temples beat like sledge hammers, and I believe I would have had a fit of some sort except that at that very moment my nose started to bleed.

"What do you think of Lucy Ferrier now?" I cried, blood flowing from my nose as I locked the door, and shook the key in his face. "Punishment has been slow in coming, but it has overtaken you at last." I saw his coward lips tremble as I spoke. He would have begged for his life, but he knew well that it was useless.

"Would you murder me?" he stammered.

"There is no murder," I answered. "Who talks of murdering a mad dog? What mercy had you upon my poor darling, when you dragged her from her slaughtered father, and bore her away to your accursed and shameless harem?"

"I was not the one who killed her father," he cried.

"But it was you who broke her innocent heart,"

I shrieked, thrusting the box before him. "Let the High Judge decide between us. Choose and eat. There is death in one and life in the other. I shall take what you leave. Let us see if there is justice upon the earth, or if we are ruled by chance."

He cowered away with wild cries and prayers for mercy, but I drew my knife and held it to his throat until he had obeyed me. Then I swallowed the other, and we stood facing one another in silence for a minute or more, waiting to see which was to live and which was to die. Shall I ever forget the look which came over his face when the first warning pangs told him that he had taken the poison? I laughed as I saw it, and held Lucy's marriage ring in front of his eyes. It was but for a moment, for the poison worked quickly. A spasm of pain contorted his features; he threw his hands out in front of him, staggered, and then, with a hoarse cry, fell heavily upon the floor. I turned him over with my foot, and placed my hand upon his heart. There was no movement. He was dead!

The blood had been streaming from my nose, but I had taken no notice of it. I don't know what it was that put it into my head to write upon the wall with it. Perhaps it was some mischievous idea of setting the police upon a wrong track, for I felt light hearted and cheerful. I remembered a German being found in New York with RACHE written up above him, and it was argued at the time in the newspapers that the secret societies must have done it. I guessed that what puzzled the New Yorkers would puzzle the Londoners, so I dipped my finger in my own blood and printed it on a convenient place on the wall. Then I walked down to my cab and found that there was nobody about, and that the night was still very wild. I had driven some distance when I put my hand into the pocket in which I usually kept Lucy's ring, and found that it was not there. I was shocked at this, for it was the only memento I had of her. Thinking that I might have dropped it when I stooped over Drebber's body, I drove back, and leaving my cab in a side street, I went boldly up to the house—for I was ready to dare anything rather than lose the ring. When I arrived there, I walked right into the arms of a police officer who was coming out, and only managed to disarm his suspicions by pretending to be hopelessly drunk.

That was how Enoch Drebber came to his end. All I had to do then was do the same to Stangerson, and so pay off John Ferrier's debt. I knew that he was staying at Halliday's Private Hotel, and I hung about all day, but he never came out. I guess that he suspected something when Drebber failed to put in an appearance. He was cunning, was Stangerson, and always on his guard. If he thought he could keep me off by staying indoors he was very much mistaken. I soon found out which was the window of his bedroom. Early the next morning I took advantage of some ladders which were lying in the lane behind the hotel, and so made my way into his room in the grey of the dawn. I woke him up and told him that the hour had come when he was to answer for the life he had taken so long before. I described Drebber's death to him, and I gave him the same choice of the poisoned pills. Instead of grasping at the chance of safety that was offered him, he sprang from his bed and reached for my throat. In self-defense I stabbed him to the heart. It would have been the same in any case, for Providence would never have allowed his guilty hand to pick out anything but the poison.

    I have little more to say, and it's as well, for I am exhausted. I went on cabbing it for a day or so, intending to keep at it until I could save enough to take me back to America. I was standing in the yard when a ragged youngster asked if there was a cabby there called Jefferson Hope, and said that his cab was wanted by a gentleman at 221B, Baker Street. I went round, suspecting no harm, and the next thing I knew, this young man here had the bracelets on my wrists, and as neatly snackled as ever I saw in my life. That's the whole of my story, gentlemen. You may consider me to be a murderer; but I hold that I am just as much an officer of justice as you are.

CHAPTER XII.
THE CONCLUSION

SO thrilling had the man's narrative been, and his manner so impressive that we had all sat silent and absorbed. Even the professional detectives, bored as they were with most every detail of crime, appeared to be keenly interested in the man's story. When he finished we sat for some minutes in a stillness which was only broken by the scratching of Lestrade's pencil as he gave the finishing touches to his shorthand account.

"There is only one point on which I should like a little more information," Sherlock Holmes said at last. "Who was your accomplice who came for the ring which I advertised?"

The prisoner winked at my friend. "I can tell my own secrets," he said, "but I don't get other people into trouble. I saw your advertisement, and I thought it might be a trap, or it might be the ring which I wanted. My friend volunteered to go and see. I think you'll own he did it smartly."

"Not a doubt of that," said Holmes heartily.

"Now, gentlemen," the Inspector remarked gravely, "the forms of the law must be complied with.

On Thursday the prisoner will be brought before the magistrates, and your attendance will be required. Until then I will be responsible for him." He rang the bell as he spoke, and Jefferson Hope was led off by a couple of warders, while my friend and I made our way out of the Station and took a cab back to Baker Street.

We had all been warned to appear before the magistrates upon the Thursday; but when the Thursday came there was no occasion for our testimony. A higher Judge had taken the matter in hand, and Jefferson Hope had been summoned before a tribunal where strict justice would be meted out to him. On the very night after his capture the aneurism burst, and he was found in the morning stretched upon the floor of the cell, with a smile upon his face, as though he had been able in his dying moments to look back upon a life well lived.

"Gregson and Lestrade will be wild about his death," Holmes remarked, as we chatted it over the next evening. "Where will their grand advertisement be now?"

"I don't see that they had very much to do with his capture," I answered.

"What you do in this world is a matter of no consequence," returned my companion, bitterly. "The question is, what can you make people believe that you have done. Never mind," he continued, more brightly, after a pause. "I would not have missed the investigation for anything. There has been no better case within my recollection. Simple as it was, there were several most instructive points about it."

"Simple!" I cried.

"Well, really, it can hardly be described as otherwise," said Sherlock Holmes, smiling at my surprise. "The proof of its intrinsic simplicity is, that without any help save a few very ordinary deductions, I was able to lay my hand upon the criminal within three days."

"That is true," said I.

"I have already explained to you that what is unusual is usually a help rather than a hindrance. In solving a problem of this sort, the main thing is to be able to reason backwards. That is a very useful accomplishment, and a very easy one, but people do not practice it much. In the everyday affairs of life it is more useful to reason forwards, and so the other comes to be neglected. There are fifty who can reason synthetically for one who can reason analytically."

"I confess," said I, "that I do not quite follow you."

"I hardly expected that you would. Let me see if I can make it clearer. Most people, if you describe a train of events to them, will tell you what the result would be. They can put those events together in their minds, and argue from them that something will come to pass. There are few people, however, who, if you told them a result, would be able to deduce what the steps were which led up to that result. This power is what I mean when I talk of reasoning backwards, or analytically."

"I understand," said I.

"Now, this was a case in which you were given the result and had to find everything else for yourself. Let me try to show you the different steps in my reasoning. To begin at the beginning. I approached the house, as you know, on foot, and with my mind entirely free from all impressions. I naturally began by examining the roadway, and there, as I have already explained to you, I saw clearly the marks of a cab, which, I learned by inquiring, must have been there during the night. I knew that it was a cab and not a private carriage by the narrow width of the wheels. The ordinary London cab is considerably less wide than a gentleman's carriage.

"This was the first point gained. I then walked slowly down the garden path, which happened to be composed of a clay soil, particularly good for taking impressions. No doubt it appeared to you to be a mere trampled line of slush, but to my trained eyes every mark upon its surface had a meaning. There is no branch of detective science which is so important and so much neglected as the art of tracing footsteps. Happily, I have always laid great stress upon it, and much practice has made it second nature to me. I saw the heavy footmarks of the constables, but I saw also the track of the two men who had first passed through the garden. It was easy to tell that they had been there before the others, because in places their marks had been entirely erased by the others coming on top of them. In this way my second link was formed, which told me that the nighttime visitors were two in number, one quite tall (as I saw from the length of his stride), and the other fashionably dressed, to judge from the small and elegant impression left by his boots.

"On entering the house this last point was confirmed. My well booted man lay before me. The tall one, then, had done the murder, if it was murder at all. There was no wound upon the dead man's person, but the expression upon his face showed me that he had foreseen his fate before it came upon him. Men who die from heart disease, or any sudden natural cause, never by any chance exhibit agitation upon their features. Having sniffed the dead man's lips I detected a slightly sour smell, and I came to the conclusion that he had had poison forced upon him. I knew it had been forced upon him from the hatred and fear expressed upon his face. By the method of exclusion, I had arrived at this result, for no other hypothesis would meet the facts. Do not imagine that it was a very unheard of idea. The forcible giving of poison is by no means a new thing in criminal annals. The cases of Dolsky in Odessa, and of Leturier in Montpellier, will occur at once to any toxicologist.

"And now came the great question as to the reason why. Robbery had not been the object of the murder, for nothing was taken. Was it politics, then, or was it a woman? That was the question which confronted me. I was inclined from the beginning to believe it was a woman. Political assassins are only too glad to do their work and run. This murder had, on the contrary, been done more slowly, and the murderer had left footprints all over the room, showing that he had been there all the time. That showed that it must have been a case of revenge. When the word 'Rache' was discovered upon the wall I was more inclined than ever to my opinion. 'Rache' was too evidently a blind, meant to confuse the police. When the ring was found, however, it settled the question. Clearly the murderer had used it to remind his victim of some dead or absent woman. It was at this point that I asked Gregson what he had asked the Cleveland police about Mr.

Drebber's life. He answered, you remember, that he had asked nothing.

"I then made a careful examination of the room, which confirmed my opinion about the murderer's height, and gave me with the additional details as to the Trichinopoly cigar and the length of his nails. I had already come to the conclusion, since there were no signs of a struggle, that the blood which covered the floor had burst from the murderer's nose in his excitement. I could perceive that the track of blood followed the track of his feet. It is seldom that any man, unless he is very full blooded, breaks out in this way through emotion, so I gave the opinion that the criminal was probably a robust and ruddy faced man. Events proved that I had judged correctly.

"Having left the house, I proceeded to do what Gregson had neglected. I telegraphed to the head of the police at Cleveland, asking about any strange incidents regarding the marriage of Enoch Drebber. The answer was conclusive. It told me that Drebber had already asked for police protection against an old rival in love, named Jefferson Hope, and that this same Hope was at present in Europe. I knew now that I held the clue to the mystery in my hand, and all that remained was to secure the murderer.

"I had already determined in my own mind that the man who had walked into the house with Drebber was none other than the man who had driven the cab. The marks in the road showed me that the horse had wandered on in a way which would have been impossible had there been anyone in charge of it. Where, then, could the driver be, unless he were inside the house? Again, it is absurd to suppose that any sane man would carry out a deliberate crime under the very eyes of a third person, who would be sure to betray him. Lastly, supposing one man wished to follow another through London, what better means could he come up with than to turn cabdriver? All these thoughts led me to the conclusion that Jefferson Hope was to be found among the cab drivers of the city.

"If he had been a cab driver there was no reason to believe that he no longer was. On the contrary, from his point of view, any sudden change would be likely to draw attention to himself. He would, probably, for a time at least, continue to perform his duties. There was no reason to suppose that he was going under an assumed name. Why should he change his name in a country where no one knew his original one? I therefore organized my street kid detective corps, and sent them to every cab company in London until they found the man that I wanted. How well they succeeded, and how quickly I took advantage of it, are still fresh in your recollection. The murder of Stangerson was an incident which was entirely unexpected, but which could hardly in any case have been prevented. Through it, as you know, I came into possession of the pills, the existence of which I had already figured out. You see, the whole thing is a chain of logical sequences without a break or flaw."

"It is wonderful!" I cried. "Your merits should be publicly recognized. You should publish an account of the case. If you won't, I will for you."

"You may do what you like, Doctor," he answered. "See here!" he continued, handing a paper over to me, "look at this!"

It was the *Echo* for the day, and the paper had a

long article upon the case.

"The public," it said, "have lost a sensational treat through the sudden death of the man Hope, who was suspected of the murder of Mr. Enoch Drebber and of Mr. Joseph Stangerson. The details of the case will probably be never known now, though we are informed upon good authority that the crime was the result of an old standing romantic feud, in which love and Mormonism bore a part. It seems that both the victims belonged, in their younger days, to the Latter Day Saints, and Hope, the deceased prisoner, also lived in Salt Lake City. If the case has had no other effect, it, at least, brings out in the most striking manner the efficiency of our detective police force. It will serve as a lesson to all foreigners that they will do wisely to settle their feuds at home, and not to carry them on to British soil. It is an open secret that the credit of this smart capture belongs entirely to the well known Scotland Yard officials, Messrs. Lestrade and Gregson. The man was caught, it appears, in the rooms of a certain Mr. Sherlock Holmes, who has himself, as an amateur, shown some talent in the detective line, and who, with such instructors, may hope in time to attain some degree of their skill. It is expected that an award of some sort will be presented to the two officers as a fitting recognition of their services."

"Didn't I tell you so when we started?" cried Sherlock Holmes with a laugh. "That's the result of all our Study in Scarlet: to get them an award!"

"Never mind," I answered, "I have all the facts in my journal. I will publish the details of the case myself, and the public will know the truth."

Sherlock Holmes sighed and gave a quizzical

half-smile, then looked at me with amusement. "In any case, Watson, you have turned out to be a prize flat-mate. I couldn't have asked for better."

MORE ABOUT MORMONS

CONAN Doyle's original version of *A Study in Scarlet* has met with controversy due to its treatment of Mormons. Mormons did not exist in England at the time Doyle was writing the book, but rumors of their practices certainly reached London. However, as with all rumors, what Doyle heard were probably a collection of half-truths.

In this edition, I have tried to remove or change as much potentially offensive material as possible without taking away from the story itself. I also want to set the story straight on some controversial facts.

The Mormons were founded in 1830 by Joseph Smith. When Smith and his brother were killed during anti-Mormon riots in 1844, Brigham Young took over the church. He eventually moved his followers to Utah, where they could live without fear of opposition.

At the time *A Study in Scarlet* was printed, the Mormons did in fact practice polygamy, known to them as plural marriage, which allowed a man to be married to multiple wives. This practice was officially denounced in 1890 by the Mormon church, just three years after *A Study in Scarlet* was published. In 1904, plural marriage was denounced a second time. This ban was more effective, and plural marriages have not been condoned since.

The Danites, also known as the Avenging Angels, did exist as a military wing of the Mormons in the early days of the religion, mainly to protect the people from attack. It is unknown, however, whether this group continued to exist after the move to Utah.

ABOUT THE AUTHORS

Sir Arthur Conan Doyle
Arthur Ignatius Conan Doyle was born on 22 May 1859 in Edinburgh, Scotland. He studied medicine at the University of Edinburgh, but his private medical career was initially slow to take off. Sitting in his office, waiting for patients to arrive, Conan Doyle would pass the time writing. His most famous works were the stories of Sherlock Holmes. Holmes appeared in four novels and 56 short stories written over an amazing 39 year period. King Edward VII made Conan Doyle a knight, not for his Sherlock Holmes stories, as many people assume, but for a piece he wrote on the Boer War in South Africa. He had traveled to South Africa in 1900 to serve in a medical unit treating British troops. His publication defended the British government against numerous charges regarding their conduct during the war, and the King considered it a great service to the country. Conan Doyle died of a heart attack on 7 July 1930 at the age of 71. His last words, "you are wonderful," were directed towards his wife.

Leo Zanav
Leo Zanav is a lover of classics. He launched his Classics Remastered series to serve as a bridge connecting modern and younger readers with the great works of an earlier age. Leo lives in the countryside with his wife and son, and enjoys spending his time in nature.

NOW AVAILABLE: THE GREATEST SHERLOCK HOLMES STORY EVER TOLD!

SHERLOCK HOLMES REMASTERED

BOOK 2

THE HOUND OF THE BASKERVILLES

The Baskerville's have an ancient family legend, of a hound from hell that reaps vengeance upon all the Baskerville men. Now Sir Charles Baskerville is dead under mysterious circumstances. His nephew and heir, Sir Henry Baskerville, returns to England to inherit the family estate. Can Sherlock Holmes save him from the demonic hound?

The Hound of the Baskervilles remains the most famous and most celebrated Sherlock Holmes story of all time. Holmes needs all of his cunning and conniving to break through the supernatural legend and hunt down the murder that he believes lies beneath. The Remastered version is packed with action and builds to an ending as intense as the legend itself.

Download a free sample at ClassicsRemastered.com.

IF YOU ENJOYED SHERLOCK HOLMES REMASTERED, JOIN THE DIALOGUE!

SMALL THINGS YOU CAN DO:

1. CONNECT WITH US ON FACEBOOK AT FACEBOOK.COM/SHERLOCKHOLMESREMASTERED

2. RATE THIS BOOK ON AMAZON OR OTHER ONLINE STORES

3. VISIT US AT CLASSICSREMASTERED.COM

Made in the USA
Lexington, KY
17 November 2012